A
TEMPLAR
KNIGHT'S
TALE

A TEMPLAR KNIGHT'S TALE

THE QUEST

HENRY FUSCO

A TEMPLAR KNIGHT'S TALE
THE QUEST

iUniverse books may be ordered through booksellers or by contacting:

iUniverse
1663 Liberty Drive
Bloomington, IN 47403
www.iuniverse.com
844-349-9409

Because of the dynamic nature of the Internet, any web addresses or links contained in this book may have changed since publication and may no longer be valid. The views expressed in this work are solely those of the author and do not necessarily reflect the views of the publisher, and the publisher hereby disclaims any responsibility for them.

Any people depicted in stock imagery provided by Getty Images are models, and such images are being used for illustrative purposes only.
Certain stock imagery © Getty Images.

ISBN: 978-1-6632-3194-9 (sc)
ISBN: 978-1-6632-3208-3 (hc)
ISBN: 978-1-6632-3195-6 (e)

Library of Congress Control Number: 2021923189

Print information available on the last page.

iUniverse rev. date: 11/30/2021

CONTENTS

AKCNOWLEDGEMENT

My wife, Wendy Fusco, for her understanding, patience, and support.

iUniverse for giving me the opportunity to publish my book.

PROLOGUE

The castle keep in Naples, Italy

1288

A blazing fire burned in the hearth of the great hall that evening as the regent, Mattiano DeFusco, a robust man in his forties, with broad shoulders and barrel chest, paced to and fro, waiting for his son, Prince Henry, to be brought before him. He stopped and looked to his wife, Lady Serafina, the grand duchess. Pain and sorrow filled their eyes as they looked to each other for comfort. A tear fell from the eye of the regent, but he quickly wiped it away. As a mighty warrior and leader of men, he was embarrassed to show his tumultuous feelings.

Lady Serafina, a handsome woman in her early forties, held a delicate fabric to her weeping eyes. Feeling the pain that was surely in her heart, the regent's younger brothers tried to give her solace. They were true to their DeFusco bloodline—powerfully built, mighty, fearless warriors who had fought and triumphed and who wore their battle scars with pride. All six brothers were dukes of the realm.

A knock at the door of the regent's inner chamber brought all eyes to the guard who entered. His uniform was in the colors of the DeFusco family: royal blue with gold trim.

The guard announced, "My lord, your son, Prince Henry, has arrived."

Mattiano replied, "Send him in!"

Regent Mattiano watched his son enter the room with confident strides. The prince stopped and gave a slight nod of respect to his mother and uncles. Then he stood ramrod straight in front of his father's throne. The father fought back his anger and appraised his son standing before him. At twenty years of age, the prince was tall like his uncles but not as broad. He was like a leopard in his movements—quick, powerful, and deadly.

The prince was the most celebrated swordsman in Europe and had never been beaten in a tournament. Prince Henry DeFusco was feared by all but those at this meeting. Brash and quick-tempered, with supernatural speed and uniqueness of style, he backed up his words with sword and dagger. Death had followed him. He had fought numerous duels, leaving a bloody trail of bodies wherever he went. He was death incarnate. Mattiano was both proud of and sad for his son.

Considering politics in Naples and France and his son's hotheadedness, Regent Mattiano had made a hard decision. There had been dissension between him and his brothers on his decision. But what could he have done? Mattiano loved his son but was fearful after his son's recent actions and their repercussions. Mattiano had tried to protect his son in the past, but the future was doubtful.

Mattiano fought back his anger, but to no avail. "You have gone against my orders and have killed the French ambassador in a duel. This is the fifteenth time you have killed a representative of the king of France to our court!" The political fallout was going to be bad because France controlled the kingdom of Naples and Sicily. Italy was comprised of city-states and was not a unified country. "The king of France has now put a bounty on your head of twenty thousand gold pieces. My own son! You are now considered a wolf's head. An outlaw!"

Prince Henry responded, "Father, the man was a pig. I did not like the way he abused our women. I fought for their honor."

Mattiano said, "Cannot other men fight for the honor of our women? Why you? It makes me think our men of Naples are all cowards who cannot defend the honor of women. Is this true?" The regent tried to stare down his son but saw the fire in his eyes.

Prince Henry replied, "No, Father. The men of Naples are strong. With them behind me, I will drive out the pompous foreigners and rule the kingdom of Naples and Sicily with Italians! Naples should not answer to France or any other European power. We are like curs begging for a bone and trying to please our master. But we get kicked in our ass for all we do. I am tired of this. I say it is time to fight for what we have. Why give the king of France tax money for this and tax money for that? He is bleeding Naples of our riches!"

Mattiano said, "This cannot go on any longer. You are my only son! I must protect you by banishing you from the kingdom. Your uncles and I have voted, and except for Mark Anthony and Enrico, we voted for you to leave. I will make an announcement to the court shortly. You will accompany me for my announcement and face the other nobles of our court."

The prince slowly shook his head. With a broken smile, he looked upon his mother and uncles, trying to stand tall.

Mattiano bellowed, "Bring in Sir Arturo and Sir Baldassare!"

The guard saluted, left his station by the door, and quickly returned with Sir Arturo and Sir Baldassare. Sir Arturo was known about court for his good looks. At just more than six feet tall, with curly light brown hair and a muscular build, he had an imposing aura that attracted the ladies. At age twenty-one, he already had a reputation for ruthlessness and passion.

Sir Baldassare was an imposing man. At twenty years of age, he was six feet, ten inches tall, broad-shouldered, deep-chested, and heavily muscled. He was the epitome of what a warrior should have been: powerful, courageous, and fearless. His imposing body made most men back down. The few who did not were killed. Baldassare had dark bronze skin and curly dark hair. He was admired by all who knew him and was the essence of a DeFusco. Baldassare was quiet until aroused. Then he became a ferocious and savage predator, unrelenting until what was before him was no more.

Mattiano said, "Sir Arturo, you are the second-greatest swordsman in Europe and first cousin on Lady Serafina's side to the prince. Sir Baldassare, you are the strongest man in Naples and first cousin to the prince through DeFusco blood. I ask that you two blood relatives be the prince's companions. I want both of you to go with the prince; protect him, and guide him. Counsel him, and try to keep him out of trouble. I want him back alive when all this is settled. It is a big responsibility, and I trust no one but you two to do this."

Sir Arturo and Sir Baldassare exchanged quick looks. Sir Baldassare gave a slight nod, and then they both took a step forward and got down on one knee.

Sir Arturo said, "My lord, Sir Baldassare and I both pledge our lives to protect our prince and to bring him home alive when the time comes."

Mattiano responded, "Good. I am pleased, and I know Lady Serafina feels better now that both of you will be with him. You may both rise. Let us go now to where the court is assembled."

They proceeded to the great hall in order by ranking. Regent Mattiano DeFusco, with Lady Serafina at his side, led the procession, followed by his brothers and then a dejected prince accompanied by his two cousins, one on either side. Guards threw open the two massive oak doors.

The herald strode forward. "All bow to Regent Mattiano DeFusco, Lady Serafina, Prince Henry, and the rest of the royal family, Sir Knight Arturo Guliano and Sir Knight Baldassare DeFusco!"

The family entered the great hall. Usually, there was a low drone of conversation, but that evening, there was silence.

Regent Mattiano raised both arms to the people and stepped forward. "I know all of you have heard rumors going around about Prince Henry and the gold reward offered by the king of France for my son. This reward will not happen for any of my subjects in my court or my realm upon the pain of death given by me! My son may not always agree with me, nor I with him, but such is the way with fathers and sons."

Mattiano motioned for Prince Henry to come forward to stand by a small table in front of him. On the table was a bowl partially filled with a charcoal paste. Mattiano dipped the fingers of his right hand into the mixture and then drew three diagonal lines down the right side of the prince's face, starting from his forehead and moving past his eye and down his cheek, almost to the ear. Mattiano then turned his son around so all could see the mark.

Mattiano said, "You will wear the mark of the three, showing banishment from the family, banishment from this city, and banishment from the realm, until I deem it undone. I now proclaim my son, Henry DeFusco, as an outcast. He will now be known as the Dark Prince of Naples!"

There was a loud gasp from all present. None could believe the prince was now an outcast. Suddenly, those gathered started talking at once and shaking their heads. Pandemonium broke out. A few of the court wept for the prince, who stood tall throughout the display, showing no emotion. Sir Arturo and Sir Baldassare glanced at each other, and their eyes spoke volumes of the pain and embarrassment the prince was experiencing. Sir Baldassare gave Sir Arturo a wink and moved forward. Sir Arturo did the same, and they both stood in front of the regent.

Sir Arturo said, "Mark my face and Sir Baldassare's face as you have done to our prince."

Mattiano was speechless. It took him almost a minute to react. He understood what Sir Arturo and Sir Baldassare were doing. A tear fell from his eye as he gave them the same markings. The enormity of the situation hit him, and he staggered back. Lady Serafina struggled to hold him up. The brothers rushed to his aid to comfort him. The prince stepped forward, and there was a hush in the great hall.

Prince Henry said, "I will return with my two cousins when you need me the most. It is my solemn vow to you." Glancing at Sir Arturo and Sir Baldassare, he signaled that the three should leave.

CHAPTER 1

Tristan's Cavalry Charge

I sat in a chair near a fire blazing in the fireplace of the great hall, an older man long past my prime. My long beard, once red, was now gray. It was the winter of my life in the year 1338, and I was trying to get warm in the drafty fortress.

"Uncle Tristan, tell us the story of our grandfather the Dark Prince, our grandmother Ravenaire, funny Uncle Arturo, scary Uncle Baldassare, and the old monk Uncle Danner," pleaded the red-haired Mark Anthony.

"Yes, Uncle Tristan. You promised. A man's worth is based on keeping promises," said Franco matter-of-factly.

I smiled and looked at the twins, one with the red hair of their mother and the other with the curly dark hair of their father. The curly-haired Franco spoke like his father. The boys were fourteen years old and loved to hear stories about the family back in the old days.

I stood up, wrapping a bearskin around my broad shoulders and taking a noble stance. "I, Tristan du Lyonesse, a Knight Templar and close friend of Prince Henry DeFusco, would love to tell the story of heroic knights, great battles, evildoers, and the Dark Prince of Naples, a complex man who traveled over two continents to find himself. In his travels, he was accompanied by his two cousins. This is a story I know well, for I was present for much of it. I have pieced together the remainder from my conversations with those involved, as well as a bit of rumor and, yes, in my mind's eye, a little more of a connection to the story. I hope you will forgive me for these literary liberties, as every good story needs a slight embellishment, do you not think? Arturo, the skillful one, was a deadly swordsman second only to the Dark Prince. His other cousin was the ferocious Baldassare, the strongest man in Naples. He was a quiet man, but when aroused, his legendary strength and brute force were savage and terrifying."

"A good story needs a villain," Franco said.

"We have one—a miscreant called Greco," I said. "This knave was rescued by the Dark Prince during the Sicilian Vespers. This battle drove the French out of Sicily. In the battle, the Dark Prince fought five French soldiers to the death to save Greco, who was gravely wounded. A few years later, in Naples, Greco made a visit to the Dark Prince. During the visit, Greco tried to steal priceless jewels from the DeFusco family. Greco was caught and was lucky to live through a fight with the Dark Prince over the theft. Baldassare said the Dark Prince should have killed Greco. Greco was the only man to survive a fight with the Dark Prince. Arturo and Baldassare said the Dark Prince would regret letting Greco live. The blackguard Greco made a deal with the general of an invading army in Naples to capture the DeFusco brothers for ransom. The swine Greco ordered mercenaries to kill Regent Mattiano, father of the Dark Prince. The nefarious Greco then stole the ransom the Dark Prince had paid to return his father. The Dark Prince was on a relentless search to find Greco and avenge the deaths of his father and uncles."

"What about love?" Mark Anthony asked.

"Ravenaire was the love of the Dark Prince, and he was hers. This fiery woman had dark red hair, which was unusual for an Italian in Naples; slanted green eyes; and a temperament that matched all the passion of the Dark Prince. She was fiercely loyal to the prince and as good as any man with a blade. She was incredibly beautiful and deeply in love with the Dark Prince.

"Oh, and did I mention the Assassins of Syria and their relationship to the Dark Prince? The Dark Prince was accepted by the Assassins and Tamir, their leader, who treated the Dark Prince as a brother. Tamir and the Dark Prince had many adventures together, along with the Assassins, who thought of the Dark Prince as the devil incarnate. Because of his almost supernatural lightning-fast movements in a fight, the Assassins believed no human could defeat him.

"And lest I forget, the Knights Templar. The battle for Acre on the eastern Mediterranean coast in May 1291 was the last stand of the Christian army.

"As I remember it, with the help of Arturo, the mighty Baldassare, and Tamir the Assassin, I met the Dark Prince, Henry DeFusco, and found out what really happened at Acre."

*

The sultan looked at the fortress from the outside. His huge army had stormed the fortress walls a thousand times, yet those stubborn Christians fought back with a ferocity that surprised him. He had lost 130,000 men in this siege. As he watched, he saw more men dying as they climbed ladders, trying to scale the fortress walls. He hoped his sappers would soon be done undermining the south wall of the fortress. The sultan's main assaults were at the main gate and the east and west sides of the fortress.

Inside the fortress, people were getting desperate. Food and water were running out. There were far fewer men-at-arms able to fight than there had been a month before. The formidable mangonels had taken a toll on the Christians with the continual bombardment. Defending the walls had taken many lives. Muslims scaling the walls and the dreaded Turkish archers had sent many Christians to their deaths.

Danner was resting, when the shout came that there was a breach in the south wall. He immediately rushed to the south wall, drawing both sword and dagger as he ran. Seven other Templar knights and I soon joined him.

The nine of us stood shoulder to shoulder as clouds of dust and debris hung in the air. Muscles and sinew flexed as we stood our ground. My eight fellow Templars and I represented the best of all the Christian warriors.

A mass of wild-eyed, zealous Islamic soldiers pushed through the breach of the south wall, yelling praises to Allah and wielding razor-sharp scimitars, and attacked us. Danner was fighting alongside Brother Hubert Leonce, a big, powerful man who was more comfortable fighting with his feet on the ground than on a horse, and Brother Jean Luc, a tall, quiet, slender man who had studied with several great sword masters in Europe and was deadly with a sword. Brother Gaspard Isaie, a seasoned warrior with a scar that ran up and down the right side of his face, was in the center. Guillaume, Macaire, Lucien, Renaud, and I were also seasoned warriors who had fought in most of the major battles and had felt the loss of fellow brothers-at-arms to men such as those we now faced.

We were pushed back initially, but once we found our rhythm, we held our own against the Islamic soldiers. Slowly, my heroic Templar brothers and I fought our way to the breach. Bodies of soldiers of Islam littered the floor. The footing had become treacherous because of the many pools of blood, whose sickly sweet smell permeated the air. The sultan's forces fell back with heavy losses at the breach in the south wall. Our Templar group of nine had withstood the initial assault but had suffered many wounds. We were surprised at all the carnage. We had been fighting and had not stopped to see the results of the battle of the breach.

There was a lull in the fighting, for which we were all grateful. Our muscles ached, and some of us could barely lift our sword arms. We all were covered in blood, ours and our opponents'.

Brother Guillaume said to Brother Gaspard, "You are getting too beautiful. I see you have another beauty mark on your face." We had a good laugh.

Brother Macaire was limping from a serious wound in his right leg, just above the knee. Brother Lucien, who had a bad scalp wound, and Brother

Renaud, who had two front teeth missing and a bloody left forearm, tended to the leg of Brother Macaire to stop the bleeding. Danner had a long slash down his left forearm, which kept oozing blood.

I was the only Templar without a serious wound and was trying to stitch Danner's wound. I paused and said, "Look around, and see the carnage here. There are two hundred heathens dead. We must move the bodies soon, or we will be overcome by this foul odor." The other Templars agreed, and we began to drag the bodies over to the breach and dispose of them at the outside wall of the fortress. It was an arduous ordeal because of our injuries.

William de Beaujeu, the grand master, accompanied by several Templars, Hospitallers, and a few battered knights of the Latin Kingdom, made his way to the breach at the south wall during the lull in the fighting. They were shocked when they saw that so few had held back the flood of Saracens who would have overrun the fortress. William immediately ordered the Hospitallers to look after my eight Templar brothers and me and doctor all our wounds. He congratulated each one of us and said, "Thank you for holding the breach. You have done well. God was on our side." He then turned to Brother Hubert Leonce, who was gingerly touching his bloodstained, bandage-wrapped head, and quietly said, "I hope we can shore up this breach quickly, for we could never hold the Saracens back a second time. We have no reinforcements to give you."

Brother Hubert just grunted in response as his fierce eyes assessed the situation. The grand master ordered preparations to begin for a ceremony later that day.

In the late afternoon, William de Beaujeu had everyone in the fortress who could still stand assemble in the bailey. The sky was a brilliant cobalt blue with thin wisps of clouds high overhead. The temperature was 110 degrees and dry. Drummers were beating out a military cadence as an honor guard was formed with Templars and Hospitallers. Soldiers formed into ranks, with mounted knights in their full dress colors, all facing the viewing stands. The people seated in the viewing stands were merchants, men of wealth, and women dressed in colorful dresses and parasols, all seated in order of importance. The ceremony was dazzling, with soldiers and knights in highly polished armor, pennants, and coats of arms on banners flapping in the breeze. The gaily colored viewing stands made for a festive occasion.

A small group of soldiers manned the walls and kept a watchful eye on the host of enemy soldiers fully surrounding the fortress. The host had multicolored tents going out as far as the eye could see in all directions. All was quiet on the outside walls of the fortress. Large groups of enemy soldiers relaxed in the shade of the tents or under the large flaps. Some enemy soldiers near and around the fortress laughed and jested to those defending the walls. Other soldiers nearby made an elaborate show of sharpening their scimitars for the benefit of the walls' defenders.

The grand master asked the Templar knights from the battle of the breach to come forward to be recognized in a formal ceremony. After we all were assembled, he said in a loud, clear voice, "God has truly come down to this Earth to give such strength to these nine Templar knights. It is truly a miracle that you men still live. We are all very grateful that you held the breach. Mark these men well, for they are truly blessed. If not for these brave nine men, all would have been lost. Sultan Al-Ashraf Khalil would have killed most of us soldiers and put the women and children into slavery. As I call your name, step forward and receive our humble gratitude."

As the nine of us came forward to be recognized, the people gave a deafening cheer. We were embarrassed and were grateful when, after a benediction led by the grand master of the Templars, the ceremony was at an end. We all felt we had just done what had to be done. It was expected we would defend the fortress and protect Christians from the infidels. We did not feel we had done anything extraordinary.

Marie de Bouchamps and her retinue had cheered wildly when Danner came forward to receive congratulations. She had told everyone she knew how Danner had saved her honor and her life. She was in love with this white knight. She repeatedly told everyone within earshot the story of Danner saving her. At each telling, the story was embellished. The latest version involved Danner facing one hundred Saracens and vanquishing them all for Marie's honor. All the women of the French court were thrilled by the story. They were all enamored by the ruggedly handsome white knight.

As my Templar brothers and I walked back to our posts, Danner was beset and besieged by Marie de Bouchamps. Danner heard his name called in a familiar French accent, and as he turned, Marie was instantly in his arms. Her followers all applauded and gave Danner various advice, which made him blush, to the delight of Marie and her companions. He struggled to dislodge himself from her firm embrace, but to no avail. The more he struggled, the tighter she clung to him, much to the appreciation of onlookers.

Danner was mortified and finally said, "I yield to you, Marie de Bouchamps, the conqueror of men's hearts."

A hearty cheer was heard from her followers and many amused men-at-arms who had witnessed the scene unfold. My Templar brothers and I were horrified that Danner was in the embrace of a beautiful young woman but then saw the humor in it. We continued on to the breach, talking among ourselves of women and the devil.

Marie grabbed Danner's strong, rugged face in her dainty hands and gave him a passionate kiss on the lips. She whispered, "I love you, my white knight, and will marry you someday."

Danner was at a loss as to what to say, which caused him further embarrassment. Marie finally released him and joined her companions. As they walked away, some of the young women glanced over their shoulders to admire him and giggle, while Marie blew him kisses.

The men-at-arms all congratulated him and made comments that were universal among soldiers about love and women, which prompted

Danner to say, "Enough of this prattle. To your posts! The Saracens could have taken the walls, and you wouldn't have known until they separated your head from your body and you found you were unable to blather so."

Danner walked to his post at the breach with as much dignity as he could muster. The men-at-arms laughed good-naturedly and wished him well.

*

That night, a shadowy figure appeared on the ramparts, heading for the east wall. The person successfully dodged the men-at-arms patrolling the walls through cunning and stealth. At the east wall, the mysterious figure knelt down to light a small signal torch. The figure peered carefully around to make sure no one was looking from within the fortress, stood up, and waved a prescribed signal. Within moments, a light appeared far away in the desert night. The shadowy figure on the wall extinguished the torch and let it drop outside the walls to the desert floor. In seconds, the figure had left the wall and returned to where it had come from.

All was quiet that night inside the walls. Out in the distance, a group of grim, determined men were quietly making their way to the fortress, slipping past many. The men were experts in being elusive, for they dealt in death.

*

The next morning, William de Beaujeu called together his remaining officers and said, "We cannot hold back another assault. We are down to five hundred knights and eight hundred foot soldiers. All of them are wounded, with various degrees of seriousness. We have four hundred women and one hundred twenty-five children we have to concern ourselves with. These heathens encircle us. There is no way out. I have estimated the sultan has over two hundred thousand men-at-arms to use against us. I feel it is in the best interest of the women and children to seek terms with this sultan and pray he has compassion in his heart for them. We all know what happens to our brother Templars who fall into the hands of the Saracens. If we have to fight, then let us die proud of what we have done here. The Teutonic knights slithered back to Germany a month ago in the middle of the night. Like thieves, they sulked away in the night, too afraid to face what we face now. Let the historians write about us. Hopefully, no one will forget Acre and what we did here. I will be leaving shortly to negotiate safe passage. If I do not return, pick a leader from this group—and God help you."

The grand master dismissed everyone and contemplated the future of all the people in his care. He suddenly felt weary. Running his fingers through his hair, he felt the anguish of the present and decided to pray.

Before he could negotiate the terms of safe passage, the attack came. The din of drums beating, trumpets blaring, cymbals crashing, and men yelling in battle came in a rush to the grand master. He realized it was too late for negotiations. All the men in the fortress hobbled to their places as best as they could to defend the fortress yet again. My eight Templar brothers and I were at the breach. With bandaged hands tightened around sword handles and daggers, we waited. With our muscles tense, we stood shoulder to shoulder. We realized this was the last time we would be together. Quickly, we glanced at one another with nervous smiles, winks, nods, and silly, broken grins here and there. We were ready to face death.

Within moments, the enemy broke through the shoring, splintering the wooden beams used for reinforcement, and came pouring through the breach. There were many enemy soldiers this time—fresh troops newly arrived from Syria, Iran, and Egypt. Yelling praises to Allah, they attacked. I, the only Templar not hobbling, made a lunging stab at the first of the sultan's soldiers who confronted us. Blood sprayed from a neck wound as the man fell to his knees and then died. Brother Hubert used his power and size to cleave two of the sultan's soldiers in half with one mighty sweep of his sword. Their entrails spilled to the floor. Brothers Guillaume and Macaire were battling two Islamic warriors each.

Henry DeFusco, Arturo, and Baldassare waited in Arab dress with drawn swords and daggers near the east wall, waiting for the men DeFusco had signaled to the night before from the east wall. These men, called the Assassins, were Shi'ite Muslims and would help them escape from the sultan's men, get to a safe port, and sail back to Italy. The Assassins were feared throughout the Middle East for their contracts on death. They received contracts to kill many political leaders in various countries, and they always fulfilled those contracts. DeFusco had some business with them and was extending the contract for safe passage. The men were cunning, ruthless, and fearless but did honor their contracts.

As the Assassins came over the east wall, Baldassare spotted them. Dressed in Arab robes, they blended in with the sultan's men overrunning the fortress. The Assassins wore white robes with red trimming, similar to those of the Templar knights. However, they did not wear the red cross of the Templars.

DeFusco had a quick, animated conversation with the Assassin leader, Tamir. He then led Tamir and his men, with swords held in the air and praises yelled to Allah, in a run to the breach. Arturo looked at Baldassare, who shrugged and grinned. They felt funny as they raised their swords and followed, yelling, "Allah! Allah!" The breach was key in DeFusco's plan, as he felt they could slip out to the desert from that point without being detected.

The wide scimitars' blades clanged against Western steel, and daggers thrusted in and out in a wild melee as each soldier tried to kill the other for his God. I had battled four Islamic warriors to their deaths but was slowly being overwhelmed. Danner was using sword and dagger in rapid unison, killing all who came within reach. He was beginning to tire from his previous wounds and the energy he was expending to stay alive. Brother Lucien had received two slicing blows to his arm and was struggling to hold his sword. Brother Renaud moved next to him, trying desperately to protect Brother Lucien and himself from the attacking soldiers' slashing scimitars. Brother Gaspard, his face a mask of pain, was fighting three Islamic warriors at once. He was bleeding from a dozen places but refused to fall.

Danner was barely blocking the sword strokes of his adversaries. He was feeling tired and weak from several wounds but would not give up. Suddenly, a man in black was at his side, slashing and sticking his sword and dagger with deadly precision. The man said, "Out of my way, little man. You are hampering me with your little maiden cuts!" The man in black then shouted, "To battle is to live! I love a good fight, so who of you wants to die first?" More than a dozen of the sultan's men were already dead on the ground, oozing blood, from his blades.

Danner was shoved aside by more men as they poured in, fighting alongside the man in black. These Arab men were dressed in robes similar to the Templars' but different. Danner remembered the man in black before he lost consciousness. The man was Henry DeFusco.

DeFusco was now fighting the fight of his life. The Arab men fighting with him, all professional fighters, were killing the sultan's men in wicked hand-to-hand fighting to clear the breach. A few dozen of the Assassins died. After what seemed like an eternity, all the sultan's men had been killed.

DeFusco spoke quickly to Tamir about saving the women and children still in the fortress. He would not have been able to live with himself if he did not help them. He had seen Christian slaves before in that region of the world, and it turned his heart.

Tamir gave him a knowing look and said while stroking his curly black beard, "You are learning to care about more than yourself and your needs. I think it is good for you to do so, but time is precious, my friend. Can we get these people out in time before we are discovered?"

DeFusco answered, "We can do this, but I will need some of your men."

Tamir looked at the younger DeFusco and smiled, saying, "One day your heart is going to get in the way of your sword. When that happens, it will change you forever, my friend." Tamir motioned to one of his men,

Aziz, and gave him orders. Aziz then picked out twenty men to go with him and ran back into the fortress. The rest of Tamir's men secured the area to make sure no more of the sultan's men would draw near and remain alive.

DeFusco accompanied a man named Faraj, a physician, who immediately began to examine the Templars.

Brother Hubert was leaning against a wall, barely able to stand. Blood flowed from several wounds, and his bloodstained sword lay at his feet. Bleary-eyed, he said, "These are merely flesh wounds. I am resting but will be ready for the next attack."

DeFusco and Faraj helped him lie down to check his wounds. Faraj said in an Arabian accent to DeFusco, "This man will live," and he began to administer to Brother Hubert.

Working efficiently, Faraj then moved to the next Templar. He worked at a hurried pace. Brother Lucien and Brother Renaud were dead. They had fallen side by side, with their hands still gripping their swords, on top of a dozen dead Islamic warriors. Brother Guillaume lay dead with several of the sultan's men dead beneath him. A scimitar was protruding from his back. Brother Gaspard had died with his dagger buried to the hilt in one Islamic warrior and his sword in another. He had a jeweled dagger stuck in his side and a scimitar in his chest. There were several bodies at his feet, as he still stood against the wall, unyielding, as he had been in life. I was still alive but badly wounded, and Faraj, assisted by DeFusco, worked rapidly on me.

When they came to Danner, he was conscious. He looked at DeFusco and said, "My sword strokes are not maidenly. Help me up, and I shall give you a lesson."

DeFusco smiled and replied, "I can see you are not in your right mind, little man." DeFusco watched intently as Faraj tended to Danner's wounds.

Behind them came the sounds of swordplay and men dying. DeFusco looked to the breach and saw Tamir and his men dispatch more of the sultan's soldiers. Soon it was quiet again. Tamir sent another man, Munir, on an errand. The man left on the run.

Munir, after searching many hallways, finally found Arturo patiently explaining to a woman behind a closed door that they must leave immediately. Baldassare was standing nearby and gave a shrug to Munir. The woman behind the door said she needed time to pick out a dress and told Arturo to come back later. Arturo, losing his patience rapidly, said, "If you do not open this door now, you will be talking to Saracens. They have overrun the fortress. Men are dying as we speak!"

The woman replied in a French accent, "This does not concern me. Stop bothering me. I told you I am busy selecting a dress. Go bother a peasant."

Arturo looked at Baldassare and gave a knowing nod. Baldassare moved several paces back from the door. He winked at Arturo and then charged the door, splintering it into pieces. Munir was impressed with Baldassare's strength. The expression on his face was one of surprise and great relief.

Baldassare, after picking himself up off the floor, moved quickly into the room and scooped up the young woman named Marie de Bouchamps, slinging her over his massive shoulders. She screamed, "You big beast! Put me down this instant. How dare you touch me!" All through her protests, she hit Baldassare everywhere she could strike him. He merely laughed and headed for the next room.

They repeated the same scene several more times to rescue the women and children of Acre. Tamir's twenty or more Assassins assisted. Time was against them, and they were not gentle in handling some.

Faraj, who had examined the Templars, was talking to DeFusco. The conversation was animated. Faraj, shrugging, left DeFusco and walked over to Tamir and his men, while DeFusco started pacing. Tamir walked over to DeFusco, put an arm around his shoulders, and said, "Is this worth it? Time is running out. We will all be killed."

DeFusco turned on Tamir. His hand gripped his sword as he said through clenched teeth while grabbing Tamir's robes near his neck, "We will wait. Don't think I am getting womanly in this."

Tamir's eyes flashed as he held his anger in check. He knew how deadly DeFusco was with a sword and did not want to test his luck. Even with the two hundred men he commanded, he knew he would be dead if DeFusco was angered more. Besides, he liked DeFusco and liked doing business with him. They had had many adventures together. He thought of him as a younger brother—a deadly younger brother.

Before long, DeFusco's companions, Arturo and Baldassare, arrived with the twenty Assassins. They had big grins as they carried outraged women, who were kicking and punching them to no avail, and herded bedraggled men with the heels of their boots. DeFusco said in a commanding voice, "We have to leave immediately. Put on the Arab clothes we have given you in God's speed so we can leave this place without being spotted. No one is to speak. If you do, you and everyone else will die."

After some grumbling, the survivors of Acre did what they were told, donning the Arab garments.

Marie de Bouchamps stormed over to DeFusco and, with fire in her eyes, said, "This is an outrage! What right have you to send your men and have them throw me over their shoulder like a sack of wheat? I am the niece of King Philip of France! Who do you think you are? When my uncle hears of how I was treated and what you ask me to wear, he will slice off your ears, cut off your loathsome tongue, feed your slimy entrails to the swine, and then cut off your head!" She stamped her foot for emphasis.

DeFusco bowed low to her and arrogantly said, "I have heard of this King Philip, and I doubt he could do this to me personally. He is an idealist and meddlesome in Italian politics. But I think he would thank me if I were to take you over my knee and …" Pointing to Danner lying on the floor with bloody bandages, he said, "If you care about that one, you will do as I say, or I will leave you to the Saracens to argue with them." He walked off with a smile.

Marie immediately ran to Danner and started making a fuss. Danner tried to fend her off but was too weak and finally gave up. He gave DeFusco a withering look. DeFusco gave a hearty laugh in return. DeFusco was getting great pleasure from watching Marie pamper Danner at Danner's expense.

DeFusco went to the surviving Templars, myself among them, and asked if we were capable of riding horses. Our answers confirmed to DeFusco how extraordinary the Templars were. He gathered all the people together and explained what was to happen. He detailed what was expected of each person. When he was satisfied, he gave the command to Tamir and his men that we were ready. Tamir positioned the Christians in the center of his Assassins, and we all quickly departed through the breach.

Because of the wounded, it was a painfully slow process to reach the sea. The Assassins were magnificent in protecting their Christian charges. Time and again, they would place themselves in harm's way to keep others from becoming too suspicious about the Christians in Arab disguise, who knew neither the language nor the customs and culture of the Arab world.

Aziz and his men had gone on ahead and had secured ships for the Christians to escape to Cyprus. Tamir helped the Christians board the ships and gave orders to have a few of his men stay on each ship to protect the refugees on their voyage to Cyprus.

DeFusco stood next to Tamir as the people boarded the ships. He gazed out to sea, deep in thought. Baldassare was nearby, skipping flat stones across the surface of the sea. Arturo sat on the warm sand by the shore, counting the number of skips the stones made from Baldassare's mighty side-armed throws.

"That was a better one. I counted fifteen skips," Arturo said as he picked through the sand within arm's reach, looking for colorful shells. Baldassare grinned and winked and then prepared to launch another stone.

Tamir put a hand on DeFusco's broad shoulder and said, "You appear to have the weight of the world on your back. Borrow one of my camels. It will help."

DeFusco came out of his deep reverie and gave a quick smile to Tamir.

Tamir said, "These stupid Christians owe you their lives. Why did you do this for such ungrateful people? Acre was too strong a fortress to be defeated if the Franks had only been united. The English wouldn't help the French. The Germans hated the English. The Templar knights fought for the English, the French, the Italians, and the Germans. Look what happened to them. Sultan Al-Ashraf Khalil puts to death all Templars and ransoms the Frankish knights and nobles. The rest are put into slavery. Those Templar knights you rescued are the only Templars who still live."

DeFusco replied, "I thought I could make a difference in all this madness. I want to thank you, my friend, for all the trouble I have put you through." He looked into the sparkling, warm eyes of Tamir.

The other looked into the troubled eyes of his friend and smiled. "This was a good fight we fought together, yes?"

DeFusco broke into a big smile.

Tamir said, "DeFusco, I love you as a brother—a very bad, dangerous brother. We are of the same spirit, you and I. Take care of yourself, and if you ever need me, you know how to contact me. My sword is ever at your disposal. I give you this present." He handed DeFusco a cloth bag that was well worn but serviceable.

DeFusco looked from Tamir to the package, not sure what was inside. He tentatively put a hand inside and felt something of cloth. Gently, he pulled it out. The cloth had been folded many times and looked as if it had seen better days. As DeFusco unfolded it, he looked at Tamir in surprise and said, "Why am I given this?"

Tamir smiled and put a hand on DeFusco's shoulder, gripping it to emphasize his feelings. "You deserve it. You fought like a lion for these people and brought them safely out of a storm of death to paradise."

They both looked at the Templar flag that had flown over Acre for so long. DeFusco was touched by the wonderful but somber memory of what Acre once had been. He gently folded it and put it back inside the cloth bag.

DeFusco and Tamir took each other's arm in the universal warrior's grip as a gesture of fidelity. DeFusco looked Tamir in the eye and gave his thanks once again. He then turned and called out to Arturo and Baldassare to join him as he headed for the nearest ship. The three companions boarded the ship and went to the side that overlooked the pier.

Tamir and his men were mounted on sleek, high-spirited Arabian horses. The sight of scimitars flashing in the brilliant sunshine; piercing black eyes that missed nothing; long, wind-swept black hair under Arab headdresses; faces partially shielded by beards and kaftans; and high-spirited horses milling around sent everyone on the dock scurrying for cover. The people of the harbor recognized the men as the Assassins and were deathly afraid of them. The Assassins were hardened, fierce men who traded in death. The nations of Islam knew the Assassins were the deadliest men in the Middle East. No one could stop an Assassin from doing his deadly deed.

Tamir gave an order, and he and his followers maneuvered their horses to form a line on the dock, facing DeFusco. With their remarkable horsemanship, the men put their horses through intricate maneuvers similar to a crack military drill team. By gestures and word of mouth, the people of the harbor all stopped what they were doing to see the great display of horsemanship. They gave deafening cheers and applauded them for each seemingly impossible maneuver. Those on ships in the harbor looked to the dock to admire a sight seldom seen by men of the sea—the disciplined men and their magnificent horses. At the end of their performance, Tamir gave an order, and the men leaped down from their mounts and stood at attention, resting their perpendicular scimitars against their front shoulders, while their horses were made to bow down at precisely the same time. DeFusco felt honored and returned a salute to Tamir and his men.

Tamir and his men returned a hearty shout to DeFusco and remounted in unison. Tamir gave an order, and with their scimitars raised high, the men spurred their high-stepping horses into a full gallop and thundered off the dock and into the desert. Sailors went back to work, securing lines and checking the sails as preparation to get underway resumed.

DeFusco, Arturo, and Baldassare found a place on deck that was not in the way. They watched sailors scurry around and climb up and down rigging as the ships headed out to sea. It was a beautiful day. The sea was calm and sparkling from the brilliant sunshine overhead. There was a slight breeze in the clean, fragrant, salty air. Overhead, gulls swooped and dove for fish and food thrown to them by passengers and sailors alike. It was a great day to be alive.

*

"Before that, I can only repeat rumors and hearsay of the Dark Prince's adventures with the Assassins. You would have to ask Tamir, their leader. I doubt he will say anything to you. You take your life in your hands with that one.

"One day I received an exhausted rider on a badly lathered horse. The man was dressed in black, and I knew him to be an Assassin. He told me he had gone through five horses, riding day and night, to find me. The Dark Prince was asking if I could bring Templar cavalry to help him get the French out of Naples. He wanted me to bring my men as soon as I could sail from Scotland."

The twin boys said, "Tell us more! Tell us more!"

"What happened next, Uncle Tristan?" Mark Anthony added.

I had to sit down, as I was tired of standing. "Mark Anthony, add some more logs to the fire. Franco, my throat is dry. Fetch me some wine so that I may continue. And bring a glass to pour the wine into."

The twins did as they were told and sat by my feet. Franco said, "Please, Uncle Tristan, continue."

*

There were distant sounds of steel ringing against steel and of men yelling and screaming as I rode over the rise. Down below me in the valley, two great armies were fighting. I looked to see which banners and devices on flags I recognized.

I spotted the banner of the standing lion. The lion, wearing a crown, was the color of gold on a royal-blue background. Its fangs and outstretched claws depicted red blood dripping from them. The banner of the standing lion was the family crest of the house of DeFusco.

In the forefront, I saw the Dark Prince of Naples, the most magnificent swordsman in the Christian kingdoms from tournaments won. I recognized his silver-and-gold chain mail and the way he moved. To the right of him was the second-greatest swordsman in Italy, Sir Arturo Guliano, who was first cousin to the prince and his protector. On the other side of the prince was a large knight. I could see the great power he possessed by the sheer force he used in dispatching his foes. The big man was the mighty Sir Baldassare DeFusco, the strongest man in Naples and also first cousin and protector of the prince.

Oh, how the three of them loved to be in battle. The prince once had told me that the only time he truly felt alive was in battle. He was born for war. Many men who had seen him in battle said he became supernatural. The Assassins said he became the devil. I had seen firsthand the incredible fighting he displayed, which no normal man could have done. His family crest carried the motto "To battle is to live."

I was the leader of two hundred fifty Templar cavalry I had brought from Scotland at the request of my brother Templar knight Sir Danner du Montfort, adviser to the Dark Prince. We skirted a ridge so as not to be seen. We would attack from the rear of the enemy if all went well. We made our way slowly down to the place I had picked and formed up for battle. When the knights were in position, I turned to them and prayed aloud: "God, bless these men, and bless all the warriors from Naples, especially the prince of Naples, known to you, Lord, as the Dark Prince,

Henry DeFusco. Amen." I then gave the command "Let loose the demon of death!"

With lance tips gleaming in the afternoon sun, we charged into the rear of the French army. We attacked at least a thousand foot soldiers and several knights. I felt a jolt up my shoulder as my lance hit flesh and bone. There was chaos everywhere as we charged through the French, leaving death in our wake. We joined up into our battle formation and charged into the French lines. On the third charge, we used our swords, as our war lances were broken after the second charge.

The steel-on-steel ringing of swords in battle was like music to my ears. On my horse, I approached a knot of bloodied and battered but defiant French soldiers. I shouted out, "Surrender or die!" The French did not surrender, and I was forced to dispatch them. I felt bad, for they had no chance against a knight like me. But war was hell, and that was the way of it.

There were no French standing after I fought the fourteen French soldiers. My warhorse trampled, kicked, and stomped those I could not reach with my sword. I was a strong man, but there were many French I had to dispatch that day. My sword arm was weary from all the hacking, slicing, and skewering of the French in my path.

The sun had dropped in the sky, and the battle was over. Large flocks of birds circled overhead, waiting to feast, as I made my way through the carnage. Blood and gore covered me as I checked on my men. They had all survived, though some had minor injuries. We hailed one another, laughing, joking, and congratulating one another. It was our way to relieve the near-death experiences of battle.

Several riders approached me at a gallop. A smile spread across my face as I recognized them. Gore and blood were on their clothing. The Dark Prince reined in his mighty warhorse, smiled down at me, and said, "Well done, monk! You could not have arrived at a better time!"

With the prince were Sir Arturo Guliano, the mighty Sir Baldassare DeFusco, and a knight in black on a high-spirited, magnificent black charger. The purple glint of the knight's sword hilt and his posture on the horse told me he was my brother Templar knight Sir Danner du Montfort. The men were all in their early twenties, as was I.

We hailed one another on the battlefield. It seemed we were together only when there was a battle to be fought. I remembered the good times I had had as a lad. My father was King Meliodas. He ruled an island kingdom that was beautiful and enchanting. I had grown up by the sea and knew her intimately. I had learned to sail, catch fish, and swim and had watched the sun sink into the sea. My mother, Queen Isabella, and I had taken long walks by the sea, gathering all manner of colored shells. She had made me seashell necklaces. Those had been happy times. As I had grown older and learned to be a warrior, I had realized some men were greedy and tried to take what was not theirs to take. I had made a vow to make right men's follies and protect the innocent. I did not have the finesse of a great swordsman like the Dark Prince, Sir Arturo, or Sir Danner. I was more of a basher. I was taller than the prince but not as tall as Sir Baldassare. My red hair and beard marked me as slightly undisciplined and impetuous. I had fought beside the prince at Acre in the Arabian Desert and in the battle for Naples. I was there again to fight for the prince, this time to the north of Naples.

The Dark Prince was tall and lean, with loose black curls and a hint of red that touched his shoulders. He had olive skin that turned a copper color in the sun. The prince had a catlike quality in his movements and was the deadliest man I knew. He was supernatural in a fight or in combat. His friends the Assassins believed he transformed into the devil. The prince had no equal on earth. He strode through life, and death followed, churning in his wake. Among friends, he was at ease and had a good sense of humor. His rugged good looks made women's heads turn, but he only had eyes for Ravenaire. The Dark Prince believed Italy should be controlled by Italians and not by foreign powers. Naples had been controlled by the Germans under Frederick Barbarossa, the holy Roman emperor who had lived from

AD 1122 to 1190. After the Germans had come the French in the House of Anjou-Durazzo, and it looked as if Spain would have a say in the kingdom of Naples in the near future.

The Dark Prince was the son of Mattiano DeFusco, regent of Naples, who had forced him into exile for his duels with the various French dignitaries who visited Naples on official business from the French king, Philip the Fair. The prince wanted Naples to be controlled by Italians, not by foreigners. Regent Mattiano felt it was all right for foreigners to control Italy, because they did not understand the Italian way and would be out of touch with the real power that ran Italy.

Sir Arturo was first cousin to the Dark Prince on his mother's side. He was the golden boy of the Guliano side of the family, all of whom had fair skin. Their wealth came from the trade and commerce of Naples. Almost as tall as the prince, he had golden-red hair and broad shoulders. His blue eyes were captivating. Sir Arturo and the prince had grown up almost as brothers. They were close and anticipated each other's thoughts. Sir Arturo had sworn to protect the prince on a fidelity pledge to the regent of Naples, Mattiano DeFusco, father to the prince.

Sir Baldassare, being a DeFusco, had the olive skin of the prince and the broad shoulders, deep chest, and loose dark brown curls of the family. The DeFusco clan, as we said in the islands near Scotland, were mighty warriors. They were a fearless, brave, self-asserting, hot-tempered family. They all had the dark features, physique, temperament, and curly dark hair that marked them as DeFuscos. They all had antisocial characteristics, except for the prince. Sir Baldassare was taller than I and almost a hundred pounds of muscle heavier than I. In battle, he was as fearless as the prince but had an animalistic ferocity that enabled him to kill many men quickly, leaving body parts strewn about. Baldassare loved to eat. He would eat an entire wild boar cooked over an open flame and consume four or five bottles of wine and three loaves of bread. I saw him do so several times and was always amazed. When not in battle, Sir Baldassare was a quiet man with a sense of humor. He was inseparable from the prince and Sir Arturo. He had made the same pledge of fidelity to the regent of Naples, Mattiano DeFusco, father to the Dark Prince.

Sir Danner du Montfort was a punishing, determined fighter and leader of men. As sword master to the Templars, Sir Danner was peerless. Some said he was equal to the prince, but I would make no statement as to who was the better. At the Battle of Acre in the Arabian Desert, the Dark Prince and his Assassin friends had fought beside us and saved Sir Danner's life. I had never seen such skilled swordplay in my life. It was a bloodbath the way the Dark Prince fought. Sir Arturo and Sir Baldassare fought like demons on each side of the Dark Prince. Sir Danner was adviser to the prince and tried to temper the sometimes too hasty decisions the prince might have made.

Ravenaire, Arturo, Baldassare, and I would have sworn on the cross that Brother Danner spoke with God and that a holy light shone on him in their conversations. In the Battle of Naples, after fighting several knights one after the other, Danner had been wounded badly. The Dark Prince had rescued Danner and carried him off the field of battle. The prince had brought him to a room in the fortress and laid him on a bed. There in that room, we all had witnessed a strange light and Brother Danner looking to the ceiling, speaking to God! I only knew him as a fierce and savage fighter who led men into battle but made time to pray several times a day. That was what a Templar knight did.

Then there were the Assassins—the deadliest men one would never have wanted to meet. They came from Syria and were paid their weight in gold for their work. The Dark Prince had become friendly with Tamir and his Assassins in the early years of his banishment. They had become fast friends and been involved in many adventures, so I had been told. The Dark Prince had proven his mettle with the Assassins back then. He had learned their ways and gained the Assassins' respect. In the battle for Acre in the Middle East, the Assassins, led by Tamir, and the prince, Arturo,

Baldassare, the last of the Crusaders, and Templar knights had fought alongside one another against the sultan Saladin's Muslim army.

The Dark Prince had signaled the Assassins by torchlight in the middle of the night. The four hundred Assassins had infiltrated the Muslim army of 350,000 who were surrounding the fortress of Acre. The Assassins had scaled the walls of Acre without being detected and had hidden with the Dark Prince until the final attack. For every Assassin who had died that day, fifteen of the enemy had died. They had protected the remaining Christians along with Tamir and the Dark Prince, battling all the way until everyone reached a seaport. From the seaport, they had sailed to Cyprus and safety. The Assassins were in awe of him. They felt the prince was to be respected and feared, and they would fight for him.

*

Brother Danner lifted his visor, and I saw a big smile on his face. "Brother Tristan, I see you received my letter. It is good to see you."

I smiled and said, "My lord prince, Brother Danner, Sir Arturo, and Sir Baldassare, I am honored. I came as fast as I could with my fellow knights. I am glad I could be of service."

The prince was still smiling as he said, "What say you, monk, to come to my command post after your men are settled? I have matters to speak of, and I would like your advice, along with that of these protectors of mine." He pushed Sir Arturo into Sir Baldassare and almost unhorsed them. Their horses started milling around in confusion as the prince laughed and spurred his horse away.

Brother Danner just smiled and shook his head as his horse reacted to the commotion. He said, "I do not know which is more the challenge: fighting the enemies of the prince or dealing with the prince himself!"

We all laughed as my companions led me to the prince. We made our way through the carnage. I asked Brother Danner, "How many of the French do you think have survived this battle? I have come late to the fight with my fellow Templar knights and have shattered the rear of the French army."

"Sir Tristan, is not the red of your hair a reminder of the bloodletting you do? Once Brother Tristan joins in battle, it seems he never has enough of it!" replied Brother Danner. Sir Arturo and the mighty Sir Baldassare both laughed as we all carefully guided our horses through fallen bodies and pieces of armor.

Sir Arturo said, "I remember a fortress in the desert called Acre, where we all were together in battle. I remember the Battle of Naples, where we again were together fighting the Germans. Sir Tristan and Sir Danner, you both fought well. Sir Baldassare thought we might make you both our adopted little Italian cousins, and maybe you will look and be as princely as we are!"

I said, "To tell you the truth, I like my features. To be Italian, I cannot even contemplate. They are too emotional and hot-tempered and do not plan anything—they just do it. And I like my red hair. Besides, I do not want to be short!"

Brother Danner tried to stifle a laugh.

Sir Arturo replied, "Let us see which one of us can arrive at that lone tree first. I will show you Italian horsemanship. You will see the rear end of my Italian horse and that of my Italian ass. What say you?"

I immediately spurred my horse forward, and the race was on. The tree was about a half mile away, and Sir Arturo was confident he would win. Suddenly, Brother Danner passed him. The magnificent black stallion was a desert-bred horse and had been promised to Sultan Saladin.

The Dark Prince had given the horse to Brother Danner in Cyprus when they fled the fall of Acre, the last Christian stronghold in the Middle East. An old Arab horse trader had purchased the horse for the sultan but had not yet delivered the stallion. The Arab trader had not wanted to deal with the prince, until the prince showed him a small sack of gold coins. The stallion had been trained as a warhorse. It did not fear the lance or sword and used its hooves and body as weapons. The desert horses were all bred for speed and endurance and had extreme devotion to their masters.

Brother Danner was still in the lead. Sir Arturo flew past with a big grin on his face. His pants were lowered, and he stood to show his buttocks as he passed me. But he was not catching up to Brother Danner. Sir Baldassare was closing in on me. I felt I had been a little too confident in the race. By the time my horse reached our destination, the others were already waiting for me.

"What say you now, monk?" asked Sir Arturo, laughing.

"How do you say in Italian, 'I am a humble Italian'?" I said.

Sir Arturo replied, "*Io sono un umile Italiano.* Practice saying it."

CHAPTER 2

TRISTAN IS SURPRISED

After I saw to my men, had the wounded cared for, and saw to it that they were settled with guards posted, I was brought to the Dark Prince's command tent, where his military leaders were gathered. Sir Arturo and Sir Baldassare left me to see friends, and the prince beckoned Brother Danner with a slight wave of the hand. I felt a presence behind me and turned to see the beautiful face of Ravenaire looking at me.

My face turned red as I stammered, "M-m-my lady, it is good to see you again." I bowed to her, feeling awkward.

Ravenaire laughed. "Welcome, monk. Good timing with your knights. My prince and I were worried you would not come in time." She cocked her head as she studied me. "You are blushing! How is it that a big, powerful man can fight in battle yet be so shy with a woman? What say you, monk?"

"My lady, I am but a poor monk, not used to women. I would rather fight five Saracens than have these conversations."

Ravenaire was the Dark Prince's woman and the most beautiful woman I had ever seen in my twenty years. She had fiery red hair that fell in loose curls down her back. Her slanted green eyes were alive and sparkling when she was happy. But when she was angry, they flashed a fire that would have made the bravest knight tremble. She had a wide, sensuous mouth and brilliant white teeth. Ravenaire's body language spoke volumes—a simple shrug, a glance, a smile, a raised eyebrow, and a certain look that went right through me. It was so Italian and so her. My heart beat fast when I saw and thought of her.

She was as deadly with a blade as most knights. Her temper was legendary and the equal of the prince's. She was the perfect match for him. Ravenaire was a tempest in a teacup. Any other suitor who showed designs for Ravenaire would answer to the Dark Prince. She was only interested in the prince and had dissuaded a few knights, leaving scars from a dagger she carried, when the prince was away. No one would attempt to have designs on Ravenaire with the prince nigh, for the prince was certain death to any and all. Everyone knew that. He wanted to finish the business with the French before he made plans to marry. For now, they were engaged.

"We will talk later, monk." Ravenaire abruptly turned and walked to her prince, who welcomed her with a big smile.

I found a quiet place in the command tent and observed the animated conversations from a short distance. Brother Danner was in a conversation with a knight who was captain of the home guard of the Dark Prince.

Danner du Montfort was physically powerful. He was twenty years of age, tall and muscular, with deep blue eyes and golden hair. Some said he was so deadly with a blade that he was equal to or even better than the prince. A former knight for hire and later blade master for the Templar knights, he was a close adviser to the prince.

Sir Danner was the son of Count Simon du Montfort, who had been right hand and vicar-general to Charles of Anjou in Tuscany. Brother Templar knight Danner du Montfort had danced with death many times and had shown he was its master. Brother Danner was my close friend and mentor. I thought back to the Battle of Naples. The battle had raged inside the fortress walls, and when it was over, Regent Mattiano's forces had faced the new threat from outside the gates.

An hour later, Danner had called out to me, "Take half the Templar knights, and hit the Germans high and away on their right flank! I will take the other half and hit them on their left flank, low and to the inside of the main gate, to avoid my men from charging into your men. Timing will be everything. Someone tell the archers not to fire upon us!"

Standing before me was the Dark Prince. I must have been reminiscing about the past as he approached me.

"Welcome, monk. You and your men arrived promptly. I am surprised, for Scotland is far from the sunny shores of Naples. Tell your knights I am very pleased with them. I want to thank you for coming to my aid. Join me at my chart table. I want to go over my plans with you for the next battle with the French."

Sir Arturo and Sir Baldassare were waiting at the chart table and greeted me.

"Brother Tristan, look you to more excitement? Just like old times when we battled Saracens in the great desert at Acre and fought Germans at the gates of Naples." Sir Arturo smiled and nudged the mighty Sir Baldassare with his elbow.

Sir Baldassare was eating a big piece of cooked meat, with the rich juices dripping from his dagger. He nodded to me and smiled.

I answered, "Wars seem to follow us. What a novelty if there were no wars."

The prince said, "What? No wars? How boring. Life is so sweet near the edge. I come alive. But that is just me, monk. You have your books and prayers. You try to save souls, and I take them!"

Everyone laughed, including me. I felt out of place there in the war camp, but I was a Templar knight, a soldier of God, and as a soldier, I did what I did best in the name of God. When I was with Templar knights, we did not talk in that manner. We asked for forgiveness from God and knew that God would protect us. The words of the prince were true but carried a certain bravado his warriors expected.

"Look you here on this map. The French will come from the north. My soldiers will do a slow retreat to here, fighting a defensive battle. Then they will break ranks, as if all were lost, here. My archers will be on both sides of the defile with my knights and your knights, with the French between us. After the archers' volleys, I will give the signal for us to attack. This trap will be a killing field of the French. What say you?"

I studied the map and could see no fault in his plan. "It is a well-thought-out plan. I find no flaw in this, sire."

"Good, monk. Be ready to march midday tomorrow. We will be in place in four days and kill some French."

Everyone cheered and was happy, including me. The prince had an infectious smile and could at times be warm and charming. His men believed in him, and that was all that mattered.

Later, servants brought much food and wine. I was not used to having so much of anything and was in awe of it all. There was music, and people were dancing. Everyone was relaxed and seemed to be having a good time. I turned to find a place to sit and found Ravenaire, dressed in her usual black leather and lace. She was a few paces away with a concerned look, staring at me.

I approached her. "My lady, is something amiss?"

She came closer. "Monk, I want you to promise to protect my prince in battle."

I was puzzled. "My lady, the prince has Brother Danner, Sir Arturo, and Sir Baldassare. I am but a humble monk. How can I do more for him, when you have the greatest warriors in the realm protecting him?"

"Because you, monk, have particular talents the others do not have. I want your solemn pledge that you will do all you can to protect my prince."

I bowed to her, kissed her ring, and said, "I, Tristan du Lyonesse, Knight Templar and servant of God, do pledge to protect the prince from all harm."

"Good, monk."

As I straightened up and saw her dazzling smile, I felt a blow to my jaw that almost staggered me. I looked at her in surprise.

"That is so you do not forget your vow. Do not make me angry." She was smiling, but there was fire in her eyes.

"Yes, my lady, I will not forget."

She turned on her heel and walked away.

I rubbed my jaw as Brother Danner strode over to me, smiling, and said, "You too?"

I replied, "She struck me as a man would! What is this all about? What say you?"

Brother Danner guided me to a somewhat quiet place and said, "When the prince was wounded in the treacherous attack by Greco that killed his father and uncles, the prince took a bolt from a crossbow to the shoulder. His shoulder has not been the same. He and Sir Arturo practice their swordplay daily. Sir Arturo tells me the prince is not as fast at times as he was. Sir Arturo holds back in the practice, but the prince is wise enough to know this. Nothing is said between them, but the prince is angry—not at Sir Arturo but at himself. He presses harder and harder in his frustration, and Ravenaire is afraid he will put himself in the hands of the angels."

I looked at Brother Danner in surprise as he left me yet again to speak with the prince, who had beckoned him.

I thought back to the fortress in the desert and remembered the Dark Prince then. He had been bigger than life with his exploits with a blade. Everyone had been awed by his moves and quickness. He had been deadly with a sword and dagger. Saracens had doubled and tripled up against him, to no avail. He had saved the remaining Christians at the fort in Acre and guided them to the safety of ships to flee to the island of Cyprus. He had put himself in front of danger time and again. I owed my life to him.

*

In the battle for Naples, the Dark Prince carried Danner to a quiet room in the fortress, not far from his own room, and gently laid him on the bed. The healer Dominic was waiting for them. Danner was becoming alert and recognized the unkempt white hair, piercing blue eyes, tattered brown robes, well-worn brown sandals, and worn leather bag of Dominic.

The Dark Prince said, "I see you have awakened. How do you feel?"

"I feel as though my head is full of bees. I have a headache. My left shoulder hurts, and my chest feels tight." Danner was fully alert now and added, "How do you feel?"

"Enough of this womanly chatter!" Dominic said. "I need to examine Sir Danner. My lord prince, if you will leave but for a little while, it will be appreciated."

The Dark Prince grinned and said, "I will go now. I recommend the big leeches to draw the swelling down. Lots of big leeches. And mead. Much mead."

"My lord prince, I am beginning to lose my patience with you. I will take care of this man as soon as you leave."

The Dark Prince was at the door. On his way out, he said, "You fought well, Danner. Get well soon. I want you by my side. I have a feeling we will be in need of your sword arm soon." He left.

Dominic sat close to Danner and held up a hand with one finger raised. "Sir Danner, how many fingers do you see?"

Danner responded, "Two, I think."

Dominic moved closer to look into Danner's eyes. "Follow my finger with your eyes. Do not move your head."

Danner tried to concentrate and follow the slowly moving finger with his eyes.

The healer then had Danner strip down to his waist so he could examine his left shoulder and his chest. When he was done, he had Danner lie down while he crushed herbs in a bowl with a pestle. Dominic slowly added water and mixed the ingredients thoroughly. When he was satisfied, he added a few red grains from within his worn leather pouch and mixed them in as well. He made Danner sit up and drink the powerful potion.

Danner asked, "What have you given me?"

The healer responded, "It will help you to rest. You will need lots of rest."

"Why? I feel fine."

"You are not fine. Your wits are distressed. You will need rest to mend."

Danner made a face and said, "This drink tastes vile!"

The healer moved to the door and said, "Get some rest, Sir Danner. I will check on you later." He left.

Danner slowly looked around at his surroundings as his eyes grew heavy. Within moments, he was in a deep sleep, dreaming of playing soldier at his father's fortress with his cousins when he was young. Danner was in an agitated sleep. He tossed back and forth and occasionally spoke incoherently. He was obviously reliving something of importance.

*

Dominic, the old healer, wiped Danner's forehead with a damp cloth, studying him. The others in the room looked on in great apprehension.

I finally spoke. "Healer, is Brother Danner going to be well? He seems to be in battle with someone."

Before the healer could reply, Brother Leone said, "I have seen more battle injuries than anyone. Danner just received a little bump on the head. He will be all right."

"I think he is more hurt than we know," said Ravenaire.

"He is a hardheaded French nobleman," said the Dark Prince. "He is too strong. He fought a good fight. Not as well as I would have fought, of course. He will recover. I feel we are as brothers, and he, of course, is the little brother."

Ravenaire elbowed the Dark Prince in the ribs and said, "Danner cannot defend himself. Why can he not be your big brother?"

The Dark Prince said, "Because he is too pure of heart, mind, and soul. He is the most honest man I know. If I had a sister, I would trust her honor with him. Danner has more heart in his ability to get something done than any five people.

"In battle, he is simply courageous. Of course, he does not have the refinements I possess in battle. But I could teach him. He is crude compared to me and relies too much on his muscles and brawn. And he has been with these monks too long. What do you teach him? How to pray? Fight by certain rules? Love your enemy?"

Brother Macaire and I did not like what the Dark Prince was saying, but before we could say a word, Brother Leone, the crusty old Templar knight who had been in more battles than all those present combined, spoke up. "Do not make jest with God!" Brother Leone walked over to the Dark Prince and stood face-to-face with him. "We all respect your fighting ability. There is none who can equal you. But for you to be a true leader of men, which is your destiny, you must let God enter your heart."

The Dark Prince's eyes flashed as he asked, "Old man, who saved you and the rest of your monks from Acre? Did you ask God to save you, and did he?"

Brother Leone looked the Dark Prince in the eye and answered, "Yes, I did pray to God. And yes, he did save us all by sending you to save us. I prayed with all my heart and soul to God to send us an avenging angel. Our brother Templars were being slaughtered by the Saracens. And then you arrived. Of course, we all thought you were just another pompous nobleman caught up in the tides of war. But then you came and helped us when we thought all was lost! God used you as an instrument of death to save us. You could have left in the middle of the night with those heathen friends of yours called the Assassins, but you did not. You all chose to stay and save us. What say you?"

Regent Mattiano broke in. "Is what this monk saying true? You could have left but did not?"

"Yes, Father. It is true," replied the prince.

"I am proud of you, my son. It took extraordinary courage to rescue all of those people under such severe conditions. But I would not expect anything less from you." Regent Mattiano looked over to Arturo and asked, "Before you arrived at Acre, how many were in your company?"

Arturo looked at Baldassare and thought for a moment. "About twenty something."

Baldassare nodded his approval. They both looked to the regent.

"And only three lived. My son, Arturo, and Baldassare."

Brother Leone immediately responded, "The Holy Trinity. The Father, the Son, and the Ghost. The three nobles fought as one. They should have been killed in the desert before they could get to Acre. But God protected them!"

"For what purpose?" asked the Dark Prince.

Brother Leone paused and thought for a moment. "The Lord works in mysterious ways. One of the civilian people you saved; any of us Templar knights, including Danner; or a certain combination of them is part of God's plan. That also includes Arturo, Baldassare, and you, my liege. Time will tell."

Danner began violently tossing and turning. Dominic the healer tried his best to soothe Danner by wiping his forehead with a cool, damp cloth. The room became quiet as all conversation ceased. All eyes turned to Danner and the healer.

Suddenly, Danner sat up. He seemed to be staring at something in the room above his bed. A smile slowly came to his face as he continued to look at something no one else could see. An inner peace seemed to come upon him as certain brightness filled the room.

He spoke to whoever it was. "I will do as you wish, my Lord. No, the pain has left me. Thank you. I feel stronger than I have ever been. Yes, I understand. I will protect him with my life, as I would for you, my Lord." Suddenly, Danner gave a hearty laugh and said, "Lord, you know how he is. I doubt he would consider—yes, my Lord, I will try. No, my Lord, I will do it." Then he collapsed back against the bed and fell into a deep sleep.

All in the room looked at one another with questioning looks. The other Templar knights and I all bowed our heads and made the sign of the cross. Dominic the healer made hand signs to ward off evil. Ravenaire had a look of surprise and wonder. Regent Mattiano, Arturo, Baldassare, and the Dark Prince looked at one another in astonishment as their hands gripped their weapons.

*

The battle for Naples against the German army was an incredible event. The Dark Prince, with his army outnumbered at least ten to one, was able to defeat the Iron Heel, a general who had never been defeated. That in itself was a miracle because the Iron Heel had more men and equipment and the finest knights in Europe. It cost the general his life, which ended with a single sword swipe by the prince. The prince defeated several of the best German knights in single combat. The prince even rode to the forefront of the German army to ask if there were any more challengers. After three challengers in the top tier of knights died by the sword of the prince, no one else had the courage to face him. The prince gave the army of Naples courage and hope. The Templar knights under the command of Brother Danner had a big part in the fight. I was there when we lost many brother Templar knights in the bloody battle.

The Germans were already defeated by the prince. Regent Mattiano was furious with his son for his recklessness. But in the end, what the prince did and how he led the army of Naples showed everyone he could lead and be victorious. Even the new general of the German army respected him and gracefully led his defeated army home. Sir Theobald then turned his warhorse to face his German host. The German knights and soldiers looked woeful as they faced the impassioned Italian army. Sir Theobald knew that on this day, Italian passion would defeat German might.

The prince of Naples rode over to Sir Theobald and offered his hand in peace. Smiling, Sir Theobald accepted it. And so it was that two mighty warriors of unparalleled skills, who would have fought against the other to the death, heard the whisper of peace.

CHAPTER 3

RETREAT TO WIN

T he twins were fascinated with the story. Their sister, Rose Marie, joined them. She was a year older than her twin brothers. Rose Marie had dark auburn hair with loose curls from the della Rossa side of the family. She encouraged me to continue. I had another drink of wine and continued the story.

*

Midafternoon, the French army was advancing on the Italian defenders. The French felt that victory was theirs as the Italians fell back farther and farther from the valley and into broken foothills. The fighting was fierce. The French knights charged the Italian foot soldiers again and again, but to no avail. Behind the French knights were nine thousand foot soldiers. The Italian army was using the old Roman fighting tactic of the turtle— forming up shield to shield with spears braced. The French warhorses shied away from death. The French could not penetrate the defense. They felt archers were an affront to noble knights. A peasant was not allowed to kill noble birth in their feudal system; thus, they had no archers.

Suddenly, the Italians broke rank and fled in apparent panic. The surprised French thought the Italian army was fighting a defensive fight because the Italian knights would not fight a superior force. The French yelled, *"La victoire nous appartient!* Victory is ours!" and charged headlong after the fleeing Italians.

Whistling death from yard-long arrows thumped into the French from right and left flanks, causing surprise and panic. Knights and horses fell in the onslaught. Pandemonium broke out, for the French knights could not retreat, because their foot soldiers were pressing forward in elusive victory. The French tried to re-form ranks, but each new war leader was felled from the whistling death of arrows. Archers were aiming at the foot soldiers.

The volley of arrows was taking a terrible toll on the French. The four thousand archers cut the French to less than half their numbers. The Dark Prince had learned from the Assassins in Syria the importance of archers. The Turks used knights with the bow from horseback and gave Crusaders heavy losses.

The thunder of hooves and the clash of steel marked the arrival of the Dark Prince. To his right rode Arturo. To his left rode the mighty Baldassare—big, powerful, and unstoppable. With blades clashing, they cut a wide swath through the French soldiers.

As the Dark Prince and his two cousins charged deeper into the French cavalry, the Italian knights rode hard, covering the Dark Prince in the center and fanning out to both flanks. Italian steel was the stronger that day. The French started to fall back in disarray. There was widespread disorder and confusion with the French army. Many of their leaders were cut down by archers or in battle with the Dark Prince and his cavalry.

I saw the Dark Prince receive a runner from the Italian archers, who told him they would soon be out of arrows. The Dark Prince gave a signal to me and my Templar knights. I led the Templar knights in battle formation to attack the French from the left flank.

*

I looked at the two twins and Rose Marie as I paused from the story. "Did you know the Knights Templar are the knights most feared in Europe and by the desert peoples of the Middle East? It is because of the Templar training, discipline, and determination to win. In the Middle East, unlike other knights, captured Templar knights were executed, not ransomed, because Saladin, the leader of the Muslim army fighting the Crusaders, did not want to fight the Templars again."

I took a long sip of wine and then continued telling the story to the grandchildren.

*

I adjusted my war lance to fit snugly against my shoulder and adjusted my shield as I charged into the French soldiers. My Templar knights followed me as we cut them to ribbons on their left flank. My lance broke on the second charge, and I hammered a foot soldier with it several times. He crumpled to the ground with unseeing eyes. I drew my sword and regrouped my men. I led another charge through the French, slashing and sticking as I went. Our warhorses were also doing their part by striking out with their hooves and trampling anything in their path.

A French knight rode forth to challenge me. On his shield, his coat of arms showed three black crows stacked one above the other on a spreading oak tree with a green background. I charged the knight, bringing my shield up, with my sword drawn. I was in a running fight with the knight. Back and forth we charged, and the sound of steel on steel rang out each time we met. Our horses tore up great clots of grass as we fought. Eventually, I unseated the knight with a bash of my shield on his helmet. I dismounted and continued the fight. I was now in my element as I smashed, bashed, and crushed the knight. I was weary from the battle. I needed to rest for a bit.

The knight I had just fought was a worthy opponent. I was sure God had made a place for him. As I remounted my horse, another knight issued a challenge. My blood was hot, and I charged the new knight with the three blue chevrons on a yellow shield. With swords drawn, we clashed. Using blade and hilt, we battled. Back and forth we fought. Our horses were covered in lather. Eventually, his guard lowered, and my sword bit through his defense to give him grievous injury. The knight slumped in his saddle and wobbled for a bit. Blood poured from his wound. He fell from his horse heavily to the ground and gave up his soul.

After that knight, several more knights challenged me. I should have felt tired, but my blood was still hot. The knights sought to wear me out but did not know the rigors a Templar knight had to go through in training. It was going to be a long day for me.

I rode my horse to gather any French survivors by lance point with my Templar knights. Our aides had been guarding the extra war lances at sword point. We brought the French survivors forward to the prince. In total, there were only 150 survivors. We put to the sword those we deemed too seriously wounded to survive and prayed for mercy.

The prince looked over the captured French and said, "Go ye forth to your King Philip of the fair skin and tell him what happened in two battles. If he traffics with me again, I will march my armies to France and remove his head with my sword, so help me God!"

The Italian army from Naples sent up a deafening roar of approval. The poor French cowered in fear that the army would tear them apart. The prince wrote down on parchment an edict for free passage to the French to return home and put his seal down.

Later in the evening, the Dark Prince, Brother Danner, Sir Arturo, Sir Baldassare, and Ravenaire came to me with smiles on their faces. Ravenaire said, "You are not the shy, lost boy you pretend to be, monk. To slay six knights who came for my prince and then a half dozen more after is a hard day's work! What say you, monk?"

I replied, "I always keep my vows." I was not used to praise, for that was not the way of the Knights Templar. I was embarrassed and felt my face turning red.

Brother Danner laughed. "Brother Tristan du Lyonesse is a humble knight. I think he prefers to sleep on a bed of nails than to hear sweet praise."

Everyone laughed, and the prince said, "Come to my tent, and let us all celebrate our victory. I really did not need all that help from you, but I do enjoy your dedication, monk!"

That night, the tent was loud with the voices of soldiers boasting of the victory and full of revelry. The conversations were lively among all of us. The prince expressed his gratitude to all the war leaders. Brother Danner and I had conversations about how secure the holy relics were, such as the Ark of the Covenant, the cross piece of the true cross, massive amounts of gold, and the Holy Grail we guarded in Scotland. Sir Arturo, wearing a bucket on his head, and Sir Baldassare, wearing a tablecloth and a bunch of grapes on his head, acted out an Italian story I did not understand, but the prince and Ravenaire found it very funny. The music was lively, and the laughter and conversations in Italian were soothing to hear and lyrical. It was a warm Italian night, and the soft sound of insects blended in with the rest of the sounds and sights. I enjoyed watching the animated, hardened warriors smiling and laughing, telling stories, and enjoying themselves like schoolchildren. It was a glorious end to an incredible day. I said my evening vespers and thanked God I was still alive and unhurt.

With good food, good wine, and good company, we relaxed from battle. The others continued to revel far into the night.

CHAPTER 4

A Decision Is Made

Great crowds cheered as we returned to Naples after the defeat of the French. The Dark Prince rode in front of his army, resplendent in his gold-and-silver chain mail. His dark curls with red highlights from the sun and his flashing smile made the people cheer all the louder as he waved to them. Preceding the prince, the Assassins, in their black robes and headgear, marched in proud formation, playing drums, horns, and cymbals and waving colorful flags and deadly scimitars, letting people know the prince had returned victorious.

People in Naples leaned out their windows or from balconies to wave and throw flowers to him. Astride his warhorse, with his sword hilt in gold and silver by his side, he looked so proud and brave that he turned many a maiden's head. Being mounted on a magnificent black stallion made him the true hero of Naples.

The people loved him and delighted in retelling his escapades in taverns and at home. They enjoyed telling strangers and merchants visiting Naples, both near and far, about his exploits. He was already well known but had become a living legend.

Arturo and Baldassare carried the standard showing the Fusco coat of arms, the golden lion wearing a crown and standing on hind legs with red blood dripping from fangs and claws on a deep blue background. The

DeFusco motto was above the lion, emblazoned in red: "To battle is to live." Brother Danner carried the standard of the Knights Templar, a flag whose top half was black and bottom half was white, with a red cross of four equilateral triangles whose apexes met at the common center.

Following the Dark Prince, Arturo, Baldassare, and Brother Danner were the knights of Naples, wearing their colors and coats of arms on their shields and pennants. Behind them were the foot soldiers of Naples. Last but not least, I rode with my Templar knights and foot soldiers.

The Dark Prince led the victorious army to the steps of the fortress, where the royal family greeted him. The Dark Prince drew his sword and saluted his mother, Lady Serafina, who greeted her son warmly. Behind her, the royal court cheered and congratulated the prince.

Preparations for the outdoor feast already were in full force. Twenty chefs and their helpers were roasting twenty wild boar, fifteen oxen, 150 fowl, vegetables, a hundred loaves of bread, and a hundred barrels of wine to serve the people of Naples. Music and jugglers, Gypsies dancing and doing tricks, people in costumes, and little children putting flowers in the hair of fierce knights all added to the festival.

There was laughter and gaiety everywhere. At the high table sat Lady Serafina; the Dark Prince; Ravenaire; Arturo; Baldassare; Tamir the Assassin; Dana DeFusco, captain of the royal guard; Nichole DeFusco, contessa of the outer Islands; I, a Templar knight; Danner, a Templar knight and adviser to the Dark Prince; and several Italian knights who were truly heroic. Sir Jeremy MacMichael, representing one of the mighty Scottish clans of the north, was pledging five hundred men to the prince if ever he needed them. There were lively conversations around the high table.

Lady Serafina and Ravenaire had many laughs together and had much to say about the Dark Prince. Arturo and the mighty Baldassare were enjoying themselves. Baldassare was drinking pitchers of wine and eating huge amounts of meat dripping with juices. Arturo had much to say to anyone who would listen about how heroic the Dark Prince, Baldassare, and he were. I felt honored to be sitting with all those nobles. I felt humble. I was the butt of friendly jokes about my prowess in battle and my red hair. Ravenaire stood up for me, turning the joke about red hair into a masterful compliment to both of us. I blushed over this, and Ravenaire teased me all the more.

The Dark Prince was more relaxed than anyone had seen in many months. Dana DeFusco wanted to know certain strategies the Dark Prince had employed against the French. Nichole DeFusco joined in conversations with Ravenaire and Lady Serafina, who were laughing and enjoying each other's company.

Tamir, the leader of the Assassins, smiled as he observed all that was said around the table. He had the good looks of the desert people, but he also gave off a feeling of how dangerous he was. There was a certain aura of mystery about him—something exciting and forbidden—that attracted women. Men, on the other hand, were on their guard, feeling fear and certain death. He, Danner, and the Dark Prince had conversations that were varied and interesting.

The townspeople and nobles alike enjoyed the music and entertainment of the Gypsies and other entertainers—magic acts, ballads, daring high-wire acts between tall buildings, feats of horsemanship, dancing, good food, and wine. The festival lasted for a week.

A guard found me with my men. "Sir Tristan du Lyonesse, you are to accompany me to a meeting with the Dark Prince."

I looked at the guard in surprise. The guard had a stern look about him. I realized it must be an important meeting. I gave orders to my men to clean their weapons again and groom their horses. "Stay out of trouble, or you will answer to me," I said, and I left with the guard. We walked briskly to the meeting place inside the fortress.

*

The grandchildren looked at one another. Franco asked, "Were you in trouble, Uncle Tristan?"

His brother, Mark Anthony, chimed in. "Uncle Tristan, did you have to answer to our grandfather the Dark Prince? It sounds like you were in for it!"

Rose Marie, twirling her hair with a slight smile on her face, said, "I think Grandfather wanted Uncle Tristan to bash someone."

I smiled and continued.

*

We entered the great room. Inside, there were rangers with the wolf insignia on their shoulders. Those men were the special fighting force of Naples. They numbered one hundred but had the ferocity of ten times their number. They were led by Dana DeFusco, a heroic fighter from the Battle of Naples. He was deadlier than most with a blade and dagger.

The guard stopped and stood at attention. I did the same. The guard banged the butt of his spear on the floor twice. The sound got everyone's attention. The guard announced, "My lord, Sir Tristan du Lyonesse is here." The guard then gave a slight bow and left.

The Dark Prince was pacing the room. With him were Templar knight Danner du Montfort and the prince's cousins. The cousins and Tamir were standing together, watching the prince, with anxiety showing on their faces. Ravenaire was standing by a window with a concerned look. She was dressed in her usual black leather and white lace, with her sword hanging off her left hip.

The prince turned and said, "We do not have to worry about the French. They do not have the stomach to face Italian steel again. My people tell me the remnants of their army are making their way back to France. Of course, the Assassins are hurrying them along with crossbows and dagger." He looked to Tamir, who gave a slight bow in response.

We all glanced at one another with puzzled looks, knowing there was something else unsaid. Sir Danner gave me a knowing look and quickly looked to Sir Arturo and Sir Baldassare. The two cousins looked at each other, and Sir Arturo rolled his eyes.

Ravenaire approached the Dark Prince in three strides. She put one hand on her hip, wagged a finger of her other hand in front of the face of the Dark Prince, and said in an angry voice, "Oh no. Do not do this to me again." There was fire in her eyes, and her manner suggested a physical challenge.

The Dark Prince moved back a pace from the ferocity of Ravenaire. Everyone else in the room held his breath. She was almost as dangerous as the prince when angered. The prince then smiled with open arms. "You are coming with me," he said to Ravenaire.

Ravenaire answered in a husky voice, "And when were you going to tell me this? Why did you not tell me in bed last night or the nights before?" She stepped forward and jabbed a finger into the prince's chest, which made him back up. "I do not think you were going to tell me at all. Like a thief in the night, you were going to leave me. I know you too well. Do Sir Arturo, Sir Baldassare, Danner, and this Tristan, the other monk, know about this? Are they more important than I?" She stamped her foot for emphasis. "How many times in the past have you done this to me? You are a very dangerous man where death is your bedfellow! Who will be the sane one? Not Sir Arturo. Not the mighty Sir Baldassare. Maybe the monk Danner. I am not sure about the other one—Tristan. What say you?"

The prince spoke softly and pulled Ravenaire to him. No one could hear what was said, but Ravenaire responded and smiled. After a few moments, he said, "I would die for you. Nothing is more precious than you in my arms."

Ravenaire looked up at him and said, "Then why do you plan to leave without telling me? You make plans with your friends but do not include me. It does not make me feel as important as you tell me I am. Why is that?"

The prince responded for all to hear. "I am a warrior. I am prince to my people. I lead and protect them. There was a wrong put against my people and me. My father and his brothers were killed by treachery. They want this wrong made right. I am that man. I will correct the wrong and put the head of this villain Greco on a pike!"

There was silence in the room. The prince turned to the others in the room and yelled, "Who is with me? Who wants to see justice done?"

The room went into an uproar. Sir Arturo, Sir Baldassare, Danner, the other war leaders, and I answered with a shout that reverberated throughout the fortress. "We will! We will follow you to Hades!" There was much chest thumping, and we raised our fists.

The prince yelled, "We will leave soon! Prepare yourselves. We are going to the Aquitaine in France to hunt down Greco and bring justice to Naples!"

I stood apart from the rest of the men and observed the prince in animated conversation with Tamir. The prince's rapid hand gestures indicated he was saying something important to him. Ravenaire stood nearby, looking doubtful. Arturo and Baldassare were smiling and having their own conversation. I was surprised. To go to France was a death sentence for all Templar knights, but our love of the Dark Prince was unquestioned. We would all fight to the death for him.

*

I addressed the twins and Rose Marie. "King Philip the Fair of France and the pope had excommunicated all Templar knights for heresy. The pope and the king of France wanted the Templar treasure. France was bankrupt and was in debt to the Knights Templar. France borrowed much money from the Knights Templar in their battles with England and to fund their soldiers to go on crusade in the Middle East. For a Templar knight to go to France was a death sentence."

*

In the large hall, I watched all the warriors in their little groups, having conversations and boasting of battles fought and enemies vanquished. I felt out of place. Templar knights did not boast of such things. We prayed for the departed souls we had unleashed. I looked to Brother Danner, saw him in conversations with others, and felt he might be drifting away from our order. The thought quickly passed as servants brought in food and wine for the celebration. I enjoyed the food and good wine. I helped myself to a whole fowl and bread dripping with the cooked juices.

As my eyes wandered, I looked to Ravenaire and saw the worry on her face as she tried to smile while engaging in conversation with some of the nobles. She was dismayed by the battles fought by the Dark Prince and now the continued hunt for Greco, as she had hoped for a little peace and quiet. She wanted to finally settle down and have children. The prince was ready for another adventure and to face death again. *I will pray for her*, I thought.

CHAPTER 5

THE WEDDING

"Tell us about the wedding, Uncle Tristan," said Franco.

"Yes! What kind of day was it? Were there a lot of people there? I bet the Assassins were there," Mark Anthony said.

Rose Marie asked, "What color of gown did Grandmother Ravenaire wear? Or did she wear one of the black leather outfits with the silver dagger on her right hip?"

Mark Anthony laughed as he asked, "What did Uncle Baldassare wear? Did you get dressed up too?"

The three children asked in unison, "Was there a battle?"

I smiled, held up my hands, and continued.

*

It was a glorious day in Naples. The sun was shining, the birds were singing, and the castle keep was decorated for the big wedding. All the knights wore colorful surcoats depicting their colors and coats of arms over their finery. That day, Prince and Ravenaire were finally getting married. Many times, the prince had been drawn away because of war and the various battles that had to be fought. He had been banished for a time and could not return to Naples and get married.

Finally, the day had come. The town and the entire countryside were happy for their prince and Ravenaire. All the nobles from near and far had traveled to Naples to congratulate the couple. The nobles wore their best finery, accented by fabulous jewels. Many nobles were dressed in rich colors of silk, velvet, and damask. The nobles used whole gemstones to decorate their clothing and themselves. They wore rings, necklaces, bracelets, broaches, and pins in gold and jewels. Fancy clothes were a status symbol. Laws had been passed throughout Europe that forbade peasants from wearing fancy clothes, which they could not afford anyway.

I walked over to the church where the wedding between Prince Henry DeFusco and Ravenaire della Rossa would take place. Casually looking up at the castle keep, I saw archers in place. The Dark Prince was taking no chances on his wedding day. I wondered where the Assassins were.

Sir Arturo and the mighty Sir Baldassare were standing outside near the door to the church.

Sir Arturo greeted me with a big smile and said, "I see you are dressed in a very expensive white robe. I think you are dressed a little too fancy with that big red Templar cross in the front. Are you hiding the jewels of old King Solomon? I see none on you. I know they must slow you down when you swing that Templar sword. Ha!"

I responded, "I am sorry I did not recognize you. Is this the famous Arturo Guliano who fought at Acre in the desert and the Battle of Naples? I see a very colorful nobleman in red and gray velvet with jewels, a jeweled dagger in the belt, a puffy hat, and fancy Italian boots that are highly polished. This cannot be the Arturo I knew."

Sir Baldassare said with a big smile on his face, "Sir Tristan, I think you overdid it wearing that big red cross on the front of your white robe. It clashes with my colors of dark blue and gold."

I replied with a smile, "Sir Baldassare, you are wearing enough velvet on you to make several colorful tents."

We all laughed. Arturo and the mighty Baldassare were the best men for the Dark Prince. They took the honor seriously.

I looked to where my Templar knights were stationed and was satisfied. They were all wearing clean white robes, and their horses had been well groomed. The two hundred Templar knights were all armed with sword and lance in case of trouble. I looked to the castle keep and saw the prince's home guard led by Dante DeFusco. They were two hundred strong, with the sun glinting off highly polished armor. They wore the colors of the DeFusco family, including the three feathers, two dark blue and one gold, on their helmets. The golden lion on a dark blue background, wearing a crown and standing with blood dripping from claws and mouth, was on their shields.

I observed that the church was made of fine stone masonry with vaulted timber spans at roof level. The individual stone pieces that made up the vault structure bore the ceiling load and passed it into the stone columns. Slate roofing provided a surface that would remain waterproof and maintenance-free. Inside the church were stained-glass windows with a huge structural metal framework and finely worked hardwood detailing reaching up the walls and across ceilings. The interior woodwork was richly detailed and decorated. There were lifelike sculptures and richly painted murals.

The church was the center of town life. The people attended weekly ceremonies. They were married, confirmed, and buried at the church. The church confirmed the royal family and had given them the divine right to rule.

Inside the church were herbs and fresh flowers, such as rosemary, mint, roses, and orange blossoms. Garlands and bouquets were throughout.

I observed the service with a big smile. Amid the pomp and glory, I wondered if the happy couple would enjoy a blessed future. I sighed, shook my head, and focused on the ceremony, although my mind wandered. The Dark Prince and Ravenaire exchanged their wedding vows. They had worked for days on trying to get the wording perfect. The prince had even asked me what I thought about the phrasing of his vows. Arturo and Baldassare looked proud and happy for the couple. I had never seen Baldassare smile so much. Brother Danner was there with the two cousins of the Dark Prince, standing near the prince and the beautiful Ravenaire. I didn't understand why, on such a happy occasion, I felt such foreboding.

The Dark Prince and Ravenaire exchanged their gold wedding rings. Then came the kiss. It was a kiss for the ages. I—like every man in the church, I was sure—had certain feelings I would have to go to confession for. The women, on the other hand, swooned when the prince kissed Ravenaire. The two made a perfect couple and were very much in love. The wedding had been a long time in coming. The prince had put his life on the line many times, and today was his day. Ravenaire also had put her life on the line, fighting by the side of her prince. I tried to decide if Ravenaire was more beautiful in her black leather and lace, with a sword hanging off her hip, or in her dark blue wedding dress. I gave up and decided I liked both equally well.

Two days before the wedding, the Dark Prince and Tamir had searched the roads for a good ambush place in case DeFazio decided to make a power play against the DeFusco family. The Dark Prince felt that if DeFazio came, he would need many soldiers to be triumphant. The prince and Tamir had found a place where the Assassins could be successful in taking on a large, aggressive force.

During the wedding, a few miles away, Tamir and some of the Assassins were in position to watch where the roads joined together to one major road into Naples. The Dark Prince had told Tamir some days before that some of the dukedoms might want to attack on the wedding date for personal gain. Land barons were always looking for an advantage to take someone's properties and possessions to gain more power. The Dark Prince was not like that; he respected the borders of his neighbors and tried to build alliances through friendship.

At that moment, on the road to Naples, DeFazio's rage smoldered deep within him as he rode with his two hundred soldiers toward Naples. He knew the Dark Prince would be busy getting married on that fateful day, opening up a grand opportunity for plunder. He thought of a ransom for the bride. Or maybe the city would pay a ransom before he burned Naples to the ground. Either way, he would line his pockets with gold. DeFazio was a rival of the DeFusco family and resented the Dark Prince and his family for their wealth and power.

In the early morning hours, Tamir spotted dust clouds kicked up on one of the roads leading toward Naples and called for one of his riders to alert the two hundred Assassins half a mile back to be ready to join him.

Tamir stepped out into the road. All his men were in position on either side of the road, with another two hundred Assassins ready to join him. Tamir raised a hand for DeFazio to stop and declare his intentions with armed knights heading to Naples.

DeFazio saw a lone man in black Arab dress standing in the road and wondered what he was doing there. DeFazio remembered that the Dark Prince was friendly with the heathen desert people and thought this one was one of them just wandering about. DeFazio, leading his knights eight men wide, bore down on Tamir to trample him and continue on to Naples.

Tamir gave a signal to his men before jumping out of the way as mighty horses charged by. There was the sound of many arrows hissing through the air like viper strikes. Many horses and their knights died in the volley. The knights following on horseback ran into the dead or dying horses and trampled the downed knights. There was chaos as more knights and horses fell from the hissing arrows. Soon the two hundred backup Assassins arrived and unhorsed the remaining knights. Knights fighting without horses had a disadvantage; their armor slowed them down. In a short time, the Assassins had dispatched most of the DeFazio knights. They captured the dazed and slightly injured DeFazio and his fifteen remaining knights and herded them like cattle to Naples. There would come a time of reckoning with the Dark Prince.

Meanwhile, the wedding was over, and the festivities were beginning. Baldassare was wandering around the bailey, taking in all the sights. There were musicians, jugglers, sword swallowers, and magicians. There were dancing, feats of strength, horsemanship, and food. Baldassare looked happily at the food. The wedding feast included 1,200 loaves of bread, 850 eggs, seven hundred pounds of cheese, four oxen, thirty-two mutton, one hundred capons, two hundred chickens, two boars' heads and feet for jelly, an unspecified number of pigeons, waterfowl, local provincial wines, and Chianti imported from Tuscany.

Arturo was stretching his legs and admiring the decorations. The bailey was decorated with rosemary, thyme, basil, and garlic. The herbs were interspersed with the flowers, which were rich darker shades, such as red, orange, purple, green, brown, and bright yellow. The flowers included the gloriosa lily, which had the appearance of crushed red velvet; ivy; red roses; amaryllis; birch twigs; holly branches; and parrot tulips. The 1,500 guests honoring the wedding were seated at 150 tables throughout the bailey. Two hundred fifty servants were busy serving the guests and the wedding party. Some of the servants were the Assassins. The Assassins mingled throughout the bailey, blending in with the real servants as a precaution in case of trouble.

At the high table, I sat with the DeFusco, Juliano, and della Rossa families. With me was Danner du Montfort. Prince Henry DeFusco and his bride, Ravenaire, looked radiant. Arturo Guliano and the mighty Baldassare DeFusco were enjoying the day. Flowery toasts, each one more outrageous than the last, were made, much to the delight of all who were there.

Ravenaire took everyone's breath away. She was wearing a dark blue silk gown with velvet trim, and her dark red hair was piled high, with loose curls and pearls interwoven. She wore long gold-and-ruby earrings and a magnificent gold-and-ruby necklace. Diamonds and rubies hanging from gold pins adorned the front of her gown. Gold and silver metallic ribbons had been woven throughout the design of the dress. Ravenaire wore a gold circlet on her head. She was by far the most beautiful woman there. Her radiant smile and sparkling green eyes melted the hearts of the most hardened warriors. The women were jealous of her beauty.

I observed the Dark Prince and Ravenaire. I had never seen the Dark Prince so relaxed and happy. I was proud of Ravenaire and appreciated her hidden beauty. The prince and everyone else was used to seeing her in black leather and lace, with a sword or dagger hanging off her hip.

As a monk, I felt uncomfortable looking at Ravenaire. I had never, in all my travels from the Middle East through most of Europe, seen anyone so beautiful. All the men in the wedding party were in awe of the transformed Ravenaire, I realized. They were like little schoolboys falling over one another to wait on Ravenaire's every wish. I collided with Arturo in bringing bread to Ravenaire and the prince. Baldassare entered with a huge piece of venison on a dagger and collided with Danner, who was bringing a much smaller piece of wild boar to Ravenaire and the prince. The prince looked surprised at all the attention Ravenaire was getting. Ravenaire had an impish smile and was exceedingly kind.

After eating and listening to the usual toasts and good wishes, Henry DeFusco and Ravenaire visited the tables of friends and relatives. During that time, the prince spoke with an old cousin, Rodolpho DeFusco, who was probably in his late seventies. No one knew for sure. In their conversation, the older cousin mentioned his son Dana to the prince. As I passed them between tables, I heard the prince and Ravenaire assure the old man that Dana would be looked after. The prince grabbed my arm and introduced me to the old man.

"Cousin Rodolpho," said the prince, "have you ever seen such red hair and beard as this tall knight's? This man is a Knight Templar, Tristan du Lyonesse. He is French, and I forgive him for the mistake of being French."

The old man laughed, as did the prince and Ravenaire. I just looked a little foolish, for I knew not what to say. The prince and Ravenaire eventually visited all the tables, thanking all the guests for coming and for their beautiful gifts.

*

We watched jugglers do amazing tricks with various-sized balls, knives, chairs, and bottles. Gypsy dancers danced in colorful clothing. Some of the nobles tried to dance with them. It was fun, and everyone was having a good time. There were feats of strength. We finally convinced Baldassare to join in after he had finished a couple of pitchers of wine. Many nobles wagered as to who could move a wagon and how far. The estimate of the wagon's weight was about 2,200 pounds. Twenty-eight big, strong lads had tried to move it.

Baldassare pulled the loaded wagon that no one else could budge, moving it twenty-two paces. He received congratulations from all who had tried and failed and those too timid to try. He had ensured his legendary strength once again. Some of the women wanted to feel his big arms and make a fuss over him. Baldassare enjoyed all the female attention.

The Dark Prince and Ravenaire danced, doing intricate steps. The prince was light on his feet, and Ravenaire followed him step for step. There was a certain elegance in the way they moved. The crowd applauded the couple, and many nobles joined in with the women of the court. The festivities increased as more couples joined the dance floor. Soon almost everyone was dancing to the music. Arturo took a turn with Ravenaire, and they seemed to enjoy themselves. Arturo was a good dancer, moving quickly and lightly on his feet. The nobles of the court admired his style. Ravenaire finished the dance with Arturo and asked Sir Baldassare to dance.

Sir Baldassare put down a pitcher of wine he had just finished and joined Ravenaire in a dance. I was spellbound while watching the mighty Baldassare, who was six feet ten and more than four hundred pounds of pure muscle, dance with the beautiful Ravenaire, who was five feet seven and about 120 pounds. The two did an intricate dance, and the crowd went wild with applause. For a big man, Baldassare moved lightly on his feet. Ravenaire laughed as Baldassare spun and twirled her on the dance floor. At the end of the dance, they were congratulated by the smiling Dark Prince and the nobles of the court.

Templar knight Danner and I tried to figure out the intricate dance steps the nobles were doing. Danner said, "I am not sure if I start with my right foot or my left foot."

I replied, "I am sure we should be dancing with women. I do not think I am ready for that. We are Templar knights!"

Danner pulled away from me and said, "I hope no one has seen us together in this unholy alliance. I feel Templar knights are better suited to combat than to dancing."

I said, "I will not tell our brothers that you kept pulling me around and making me dizzy. You know you make me feel very uncomfortable when you hold me close!"

Danner retorted, "And I will not tell our brothers how clumsy you are and how you kept stepping on my toes till they bled."

Suddenly, we heard fiery music. People were on their feet, clapping.

I looked to Brother Danner, who shrugged. I asked people beside us, "What manner of music is this?"

Someone answered, "The dance of the daggers."

Suddenly, I saw the Dark Prince with a dagger in each hand. Then Ravenaire appeared, also with a dagger in each hand. Light reflected off the cold steel of the blades. They slowly circled each other, feinting knife thrusts and dancing. Knives clashed as they danced, and the sound of steel on steel rang out across the bailey.

Brother Danner showed apprehension on his face as he made his way closer to the dance. I followed behind with a hand on my sword hilt. Blades clashed again and again as the two dancers were caught up in the music and each other. Their dancing continued to swirl and circle; the audience was captivated. The Dark Prince smiled at his bride, Ravenaire, who smiled back. They danced the intricate dance for a long time. The two of them circled, thrusting and blocking the deadly, razor-sharp daggers. The sound of steel on steel reminded me of the many battles I had fought. I was amazed at how close the sharpened blades came to the skin of the prince and Ravenaire without drawing blood. The dance ended abruptly when the daggers were thrown at their feet, a hairbreadth from doing damage. The daggers ripped through the wood stage to their hilts. Everyone applauded their skill and felt relief for the prince and Ravenaire. I let go of my sword hilt and clapped with great gusto. Brother Danner showed great relief on his face and gave me a crooked smile.

Late in the day, as the sun was going down, men lit torches around the bailey to brighten the wonderful evening for the guests. There were a couple of big bonfires, and more meat was cooking. A couple of barrels of wine were open for those who were still thirsty.

The Assassins, led by Tamir, quietly arrived near midnight. Being Assassins, the men were almost silent in their movements. The night was their friend. Only the guards on duty were expecting the Assassins to come in at that late hour. The Assassins used the agreed-upon password, *Juliano*, for safe entry. The Dark Prince had the utmost confidence in Tamir and the Assassins and was sure no one could get past them. He knew the Assassins, not an enemy, would be arriving late at night. Tamir waited till nightfall to bring DeFazio in, so as not to create a commotion on the wedding day. DeFazio and the remainder of his knights were wearing gags, and their hands were tied. They entered a side entrance of the castle keep and were put in the dungeons by sword point, to be dealt with later. Tamir did not want the prince and his wife, Ravenaire, to be bothered on their wedding night.

*

The grandchildren all spoke at once, and I had to slow down all the questions they asked. "One at a time. Mark Anthony, I think you were first."

Mark Anthony said, "What happened to DeFazio? I have never heard of him."

Franco chimed in. "I bet he was sent to the Venetians in northern Italy, and they threw him in the ocean."

Rose Marie quickly said, "I will wager our grandfather the Dark Prince took care of him. He would do that—take care of the evil man. No one traffics against the Dark Prince. Right, Uncle Tristan?"

I laughed, drank another glass of wine, and said, "Let us just say that nobleman DeFazio left this earth and is buried in an unmarked grave with his friends. His lands and all he owned became part of the DeFusco lands, along with all the servants who could be trusted. That sent a warning to all the nobles not to go against the DeFusco family—or there would be dire consequences."

CHAPTER 6

THE VOYAGE

I was on deck, enjoying the sun, blue sky, and motion of the ship. Dolphins jumped our bow waves, as if guiding our ship to its final destination. Gulls followed our ship, looking for handouts. Some of the sailors fed them stale bread and leftovers from our meals. The way they squawked and fought among themselves reminded me of a marketplace.

A day ago, in the early morning hours, the wolf warriors led by Dana DeFusco had left the castle keep. Fog and mist had obscured their passage and muffled their sounds as they made their way to the harbor. The screech of a gull had sounded like a lost soul and sent shivers to the warriors. They all had made the sign of the cross, and a few had made the Italian sign to ward off evil and spit on the ground. Through the fog and mist, they had been like wraiths from the netherworld, wafting through the air. They had joined up with the Dark Prince and his one hundred soldiers already on board. The cousins, Danner, Ravenaire, the Assassins, and I already had been on board as well. A while later, a sinister-looking black-hulled ship carrying black sails had ghosted silently out of the harbor, leaving a roiling wake in its passage.

I was amazed at the speed of our ship. By midday of the next day, the *Black Pearl* was sailing in the Tyrrhenian Sea, twenty miles southeast of the island of Sardinia. The wind filled the black sails as the ship charged through the waves. Its sleek bow cleaved the waves as the men worked the sails. It could outrun any ship that sailed the Tyrrhenian Sea.

I was impressed with the ship's captain, a robust man in his early forties. He carried scars from fights on the waterfront from lesser men he had killed with his bare hands or blade. He was not a man to traffic with. He was called Taglio the Slasher. He and the Dark Prince were good friends. The prince had saved Taglio when he was in a fight with several men years ago. The prince had left their bodies where they fell, in an alley in Marseille. Taglio had never forgotten what the prince did for him. They had gone on business ventures together throughout the Mediterranean Sea. The Dark Prince and Taglio had visited various ports and lined their pockets with silver and gold. Enjoying each other's company, the excitement, and adventure, they had roamed the Mediterranean, visiting many ports of call.

I would have been sleeping if not for the ringing of steel on steel. The Dark Prince and Sir Arturo were crossing swords once again. They practiced two or three times a day. Men gathered and enjoyed watching. My keen eye saw that Sir Arturo was holding back a little. I felt sad. I made a vow to myself to stay close and protect the Dark Prince.

The prince was on his honeymoon with Ravenaire and should have been enjoying the days of a newlywed, but instead, during the daylight hours, he spent time in swordplay with Arturo!

I knew that pride could get in the way of some men, and the prince was no exception. He should have been back in Naples, ruling his people as the regent, not chasing after the elusive killer Greco. The prince's mother, Lady Serafina, was ruling in his stead. Dana DeFusco was the captain of the royal guard and first cousin to the Dark Prince. Dana was loyal and would watch over his aunt. Marcus Victorio, commander of the heavy cavalry, was loyal to the DeFusco family as well. The people of Naples loved the prince and expected him to avenge the deaths of his father and uncles.

Danner du Montfort joined me at the rail of the *Black Pearl*. "Is the voyage agreeable to you, Brother Tristan?" He looked seriously at me.

I noticed the way the wind ruffled his golden-brown hair. He was looking up at me. I was taller than most men. His azure-blue eyes penetrated one's body and soul. There was, I thought, a hidden meaning to the question, but it escaped me.

"We are making good time by my calculations. God has favored us with good weather." I knew that was not what Brother Danner was asking. I could tell by his face and stance.

"Have you observed the practice with the prince and Sir Arturo?" he asked. He looked down at the waves, waiting for a reply.

"Yes, I have." I paused to put together my thoughts. "I have observed that Sir Arturo holds back when engaging the prince. He does not follow through, nor does he press his advantage when it comes. I feel the prince is not what he used to be. What say you?"

"Do you know that your eyes have the color of the ocean?" Danner pulled my red beard hard, as he had when instructing me as a new Knight Templar. "We must stay close and protect him. I agree he is not the swordsman he used to be. He is vulnerable. I fear for the prince when we find Greco. Pride was the downfall of the archangel Lucifer, so the scriptures say."

"You have my sword arm to protect the prince, my lord Danner."

We both turned to watch the practice session. I knew we both felt better after our talk.

Suddenly, we both gasped. I heard a loud intake of breath by all the warriors and sailors there. Everyone, including Danner and I, stared in wonderment at what had just happened.

The Dark Prince, hard pressed by Sir Arturo, had suddenly changed sword arms. Sir Arturo had been taken by surprise and found himself yielding by sword point to the throat.

Everyone, stunned by what the prince had just done, started clapping and cheering for the prince. The prince smiled, twirled his sword, and theatrically bowed to his audience. Taglio, the ship's captain, just smiled and shook his head. In the old days, he had had many business dealings with the prince and had seen the prince take on more men than a mortal should have over various disputes on the waterfront. The disputes always had ended as if the devil himself entered the prince's body to add more souls to be tormented in the next life. Taglio once had told me in confidence the Dark Prince was an incarnation of the devil. He then had quickly made the sign to ward off evil and spit on the ship's deck.

I looked to where the Assassins were and saw Tamir and his men raising their hands above their heads and giving praises to Allah. They were all rejoicing and clapping. From the entire ship, there was a mighty "Huzzah! Huzzah!"

All the warriors knew there was no defense for the move the prince had just done. He had done it with speed and cunning. I myself would not have been able to counter the move and was amazed by it. Some said the devil helped him do it. I said it must have been the grace of God. No one who walked the face of the earth could have made that move. But our prince had. *I must search my soul and pray to God more*, I thought. It would have been easy to believe the prince had made a pact with the devil. I had heard the men say the prince, with sword in hand, was death incarnate. I shuddered at the thought and made the sign of the cross.

Later in the day, the Dark Prince and Ravenaire strolled arm in arm on the deck. The prince had an easy smile on his face, and Ravenaire was enjoying his company. The newlyweds are enjoying life and each other. Everyone on board the ship was happy for them.

CHAPTER 7

THE REVELATION

Later in the night, belowdecks in their sleeping quarters, Arturo and Baldassare discussed the last practice session between Arturo and the prince.

Sir Baldassare spoke softly to Sir Arturo. "Have you ever seen our prince use his other arm in swordplay?"

Sir Arturo shook his head slowly and replied, "I have never seen our cousin use his other arm. In all the sword matches he fought throughout Europe, he never lost and never used his other hand. I have never seen such a move as he did to me in all my years. To tell you the truth, I was pressing him hard. I wanted him to know he was slower because of the arrow wound to his shoulder.

"He really had me, Baldassare. I would have been killed if I was not his cousin. Look ye then, I am a very good swordsman. I have fought numerous tournaments and have always won. I have killed many knights in combat. There is no one who can come close to me, yet our cousin defeated me, bad shoulder and all. I do not know if I can face him again. I am unsettled by this. I fear him. I think he is the devil himself when he has a sword."

Sir Baldassare put an arm around the shoulders of his cousin and said, "You were always the second-best swordsman of Europe, second to our cousin the prince. Why does it bother you now?"

Sir Arturo thought for a while, shrugged, and said in a whisper, "Pride. I wanted to beat the prince. I was tired of always holding back. I had forgotten he is the better man."

Sir Baldassare replied, "Sir Arturo, you have worked hard on making our cousin the prince a better swordsman. If not for you, he would not have come up with his new strategy. He is thankful for your skills to make him better. It is the first time I have seen him smile from practice in a long time. This is going to be an adventure like in the old days. The prince is a new man."

In another part of the ship, Brother Danner and I were in deep conversation. During a lull in our conversation, I stared out a porthole at the night sky and the sea.

Brother Danner broke the silence. "Tristan, what are you thinking? Am I boring you?"

I came out of my reverie, focused on Brother Danner, and replied, "He would have defeated me. I have never seen a move like that. Maybe it is true what they say of the Dark Prince—that he is the devil himself when he is in battle."

Brother Danner looked sad, as if something were bothering him. "If it is any consolation to you, I too would have been at the mercy of the prince."

I smiled and said, "Maybe he does not need the protection we thought he did. Maybe he should be protecting us."

We both laughed so hard that tears came to our eyes.

In a room below deck, Ravenaire was with the prince. Both were relaxed and enjoying each other's company. Ravenaire had a big smile on her face. She was excited and full of energy. She grabbed some of her beautiful red hair and used it to make a mustache with her pouty lips.

She said, "Our practice sessions helped you today. You should have seen the expressions on all the warriors' and sailors' faces when you made that move. I thought Danner and that Tristan monk would fall down and pray of a miracle they had just witnessed. Switching sword arms was my brilliant idea. I am glad I forced you to practice three or four times a day in our secret place with me. Poor Sir Arturo."

The prince smiled and responded, "I never would have thought to switch sword arms. Also, the lighter sword you had made for me is less tiring on my shoulder. I am as swift with a sword as I once was. I am a man again. Ravenaire, I love you very much. I am glad you are with me. When this adventure is over, we will make plans for our future children."

Ravenaire was glad to hear the prince was happy and thinking of their future. She also realized how badly the wound to the shoulder had affected him. He had regained his swagger. The old prince was back!

She pushed the prince hard onto his back and sprang upon him, pinning him to the bed. "You still move too slowly. You need to move faster. You move like an old fisherman just off his boat. We will work on this. But for now," she murmured, "let us enjoy this night and forget the ills of the world."

*

Every day, a sailor was designated to catch fish for the crew. He would get fishing line, put some kind of bait on a hook, and toss it over the rail. The men would cheer every time a fish was brought over the rail. The fish came in all sizes, from a couple of feet to more than six feet long. With the bigger fish, there was always a mighty fight between the fisherman and the fish. Sometimes the fight would last an hour or more. Both fish and man would be exhausted. Adding to the challenge, the fisherman would not seek help in bringing in a big fish. There was a certain amount of pride for the man to bring in the fish alone.

One day Ravenaire decided to try her luck at catching fish. Everyone tried to talk her out of it, but she had her mind set. There would be no changing it.

A few of the sailors showed her the line and hook. Ravenaire refused to put something dead on the hook. The sailors were surprised, and one said, "This is the way to catch fish."

She said, "Bah. Why would a fish want to eat something dead? If I were a fish, I would want to eat something wiggly."

"This is the way we always catch fish!" the sailor said.

Ravenaire, with fire in her green eyes, replied, "Men are so stupid. I will show you how to catch fish." With a shrug of her shoulders and her red hair blowing in the wind, she stamped her foot on the deck. "I will show you how to catch a great fish." With that, she went below deck.

She was gone a long time. As they found out later, she rummaged around and decided to fish with a spoon used for eating soup. She convinced a sailor to put a hole in both ends of the spoon. The sailor got a hammer and a big nail and pounded the holes into the spoon. She had the man tie a fishhook on the spoon end and fishing line on the handle of the spoon. The man was uncertain of the work he had done for her. He had never seen anything like it.

Ravenaire came out on deck and said, "This is how I will catch a big fish. You do not need to put something dead on the hook."

They all looked at the strange fishing contraption Ravenaire had put together and laughed. They all had comments about what the strange, tortured spoon would do to the fish. A sailor called out, "Are you going to feed the fish with that spoon?"

Everyone laughed and hooted at Ravenaire's expense. She looked back at all the men and made certain Italian gestures that all the men understood, except me. My understanding of Italian symbolism was lacking. She then tossed the spoon over the side and let out the line. Sailors and warriors alike were fascinated. She had a captivated audience. We all waited to see what would happen.

What seemed to be a short time later, we saw the fishing line jerk down sharply. Ravenaire gave a surprised shout of excitement. She set her feet on deck and began pulling in the line. Sailors and warriors rushed to the rail to help Ravenaire bring in the fish. Ravenaire ordered them back and waved them all away. This was her fish, and she wanted to bring it in herself. The line went down again and grew taut as the fish made a strong run. Someone yelled to get heavy leather gloves for Ravenaire as they again rushed to help Ravenaire, who was now slammed against the rail by the fish.

With all the commotion and yelling, the Dark Prince, Arturo, and Baldassare came running to Ravenaire's side. Baldassare grabbed Ravenaire as she was nearly dragged over the rail. Pandemonium erupted on deck as Baldassare grabbed the line to keep Ravenaire from being pulled into the sea. The Dark Prince held Ravenaire around her waist. Ravenaire argued with the Dark Prince and Baldassare that this was her fish, and she wanted to fight it without help.

Ravenaire kicked off her shoes and gripped the fishing line anew. The fish pulled hard again, driving her into the rail. Ravenaire gave a gasp and struggled to pull back the fishing line the fish had taken. She had a determined look on her face and grimaced from the strain of the fight. Her green eyes flashed as she pulled on the line; her mouth was a thin, tight line. The men all cheered her on as she struggled and fought the fish.

After an hour of the back-and-forth battle with the fish, Ravenaire was starting to pull in line. She was hot and sweaty, and the leather gloves she wore were torn and ripped. Blood showed through the broken gloves as Ravenaire continued the fight. Arturo continued to bring water for Ravenaire to drink and to pour onto her head to keep her cool in the hot sun. The fish slowly started to come up to the surface. Everyone came to the rail, causing the ship to dig its rail into the sea. Ravenaire almost went over but for the grip of Baldassare on her.

Taglio, the ship's captain, had to tack into the wind as he bellowed, "Avast the rail!" Everyone immediately backed away from the rail, except for Ravenaire, Baldassare, Arturo, and the Dark Prince. The ship plowed and headed into the wind as the sails began to luff. Ravenaire kept up the battle and pulled in more line. Slowly, the outline of a great fish could be made out from the depths. Ravenaire brought the great fish to the surface.

Baldassare, Arturo, the Dark Prince, Brother Danner, and I pulled the fish over the rail as all aboard the ship cheered.

The great fish flopped weakly on the deck as Ravenaire collapsed next to it. Everyone admired the fish and congratulated Ravenaire. She pulled a dagger from her belt and stabbed the fish. The fish quivered for a bit and then lay still. Blood pooled from the stab wound. "I did not want the great fish to suffer anymore," said Ravenaire in a quiet voice. "He dies as a great warrior dies. He fought well to the end."

The Dark Prince lifted her up, kissed her, and said, "Truly you are as great a warrior as the bravest of the warriors gathered here. No one expected you to catch a fish with a spoon. The joke is on us. What a great idea. You must rest now. I will care for all your needs."

The men cheered and gave both of them certain Italian hand signs. I smiled and waved to them as the prince carried Ravenaire belowdecks to his quarters. The fish measured a little more than twelve feet long. We estimated it weighed about the same as a horse.

Some of the sailors, looking at the spoon Ravenaire had invented, shook their heads. It was amazing that a woman could invent something that men of the sea could not. The great fish would feed everyone for the entire voyage.

*

Rose Marie poked her younger brother closest to her and said, "Girls are just as good as boys at fishing. Maybe better! Grandmother Ravenaire caught the biggest fish in the ocean on board the *Black Pearl*!"

Her younger brother Mark Anthony said, "You struck me," as he rubbed his shoulder. "That hurts."

His twin brother, Franco, said, "That must have been a huge fish!"

Mark Anthony said, "I bet they were glad scary Uncle Baldassare was there to help Grandmother Ravenaire!"

I smiled and had another glass of wine. I continued the story.

CHAPTER 8

LAND HO

Eight days we had sailed, both day and night, and we were approaching the Straits of Gibraltar. We turned north to run parallel to the coast of Spain. There was much traffic in the area. Ships were coming from Africa to trade in Spanish ports and then leaving to journey back to African ports in the sleek and graceful Arab dhows. Mighty ships flying flags from England, France, Spain, and Italy, as well as other flags I was not familiar with, crisscrossed the sea around us. I worried that some bigger ship would run into us, but Taglio only laughed at me and shook his head. Our company of knights, wolf rangers, and Templars marveled at all the ships in that part of the sea.

We were sailing out of the Mediterranean Sea to the Atlantic Ocean. The *Black Pearl* easily parted the ocean swells. There was much excitement. Five days later, the *Black Pearl* arrived off the coast of France, at the port of Biarritz.

It was early morning and promised to be a glorious day. The sleek black ship dropped anchor about fifty yards from shore. A boat lowered and manned by Assassins in black carried warriors from the ship to shore. The rangers and some of the Assassins headed inland to make camp away from the port of Biarritz. All through the day, the warriors unloaded from the ship to the shore in the boat rowed by several Assassins.

Two miles inland, in a secluded area, a large camp was made. Cook fires were going, tents were up, and men started to settle in. We were 250 warriors strong. About twenty of the Assassins were out on the perimeters of the camp, guarding us. As warriors, we felt safe with the Assassins guarding us. Always dressed in black, the Assassins were like wraiths of the netherworld, silent and deadly. Dealing death was their trade, and they were the best in their trade. None could compare with the Assassins. Other Assassins and rangers headed out to secure our travel on the roads ahead and pick up any news. Tamir directed all their activity.

For two days, the men rested and ate. The wolf rangers ranged the land, supplying us with fresh meat and doing reconnaissance. Assassins came and left camp, updating the prince and Tamir frequently with information. The camp had twenty-five Templar knights, twenty-five knights, one hundred wolf rangers from Naples, and one hundred Assassins. To better pass the time, the prince selected knights to practice their skills with the Assassins. I did not relish that. Sir Arturo thought it was funny that I was chosen to oversee the participation with the Assassins. The wolf rangers were not to practice with the Assassins, for fear of injury or death on both sides. Dana DeFusco had an understanding with the Dark Prince that his men would not participate in games with the Assassins before we left Naples.

Sir Arturo spoke loudly for all to hear. "The monk Tristan will fight any Assassin as long as he is blind and one-armed and has a peg leg!" Everyone in camp had a good laugh at that, and I was reminded all day of what Sir Arturo had said.

Brother Danner joined me to oversee the Assassins. The Italian knights were being taught certain moves. In the process of practicing hand-to-hand fighting, the men from Naples were on their backs, with grinning Assassins holding curved daggers at their throats.

Brother Danner mumbled to me, "Brother Tristan, I am glad these men of the desert are on our side. I have not seen an Italian knight best an

Assassin. I do understand why the prince wants the Italians to learn this manner of fighting."

One of the disgruntled Italian knights yelled, "My back grows weary! Give me a sword and dagger, and I will skewer any of these men!"

I asked, "How can these little men put a knight on the ground and at their mercy so quickly?" The Italian knights from Naples were frustrated and angry that they had not bested their opponents yet. The knights were slightly bigger and more powerful than the Assassins. The men from the desert were wiry, smaller, and quicker and full of tricks.

Brother Danner rolled his eyes at me and said, "It is the tricks. The Assassins are clever and have learned to fight knights and larger opponents and survive."

I looked over and smiled at Brother Danner.

He said, "There is more training needed." It was going to be a long day for the two of us.

*

A week passed, and I was finally enjoying the Italian knights holding their own against the Assassin instructors. I felt good about that. It meant the men from Naples would be able to fight anyone in hand-to-hand combat and have a good chance of survival. Our Assassin friends were good-natured and continued to show the Italian knights more tricks. Brother Danner felt good about the training as well.

The sessions generated interest with the other knights, and each was learning the tricks to varying degrees with the Assassins.

The next day started out like any other day. A few of the Assassins arrived from wherever they had been and updated our prince and Tamir. Then they left on some mission. Sir Arturo and the prince continued their practice sessions. I noticed the prince was more confident, and Sir Arturo was working hard to keep up with him in their swordplay.

I practiced my own swordplay with half a dozen knights, but alas, I proved to be too much for them. I worked out with Brother Danner, and the challenge was to try to wear him out. He was too good an opponent to let one's guard down. He pushed me to my limits. I refrained from my physical style of punching, bashing, and stomping, for he was too smart and fast to allow it. I tried a trick or two from the Assassins, which worked to a degree. I was still working on perfecting the tricks.

The rest of the men were learning the tricks from the Assassins, and all was going well. They seemed to be bonding well. I had had questions about Christian soldiers mixing with the Assassins, but it all had been good. There were no problems of the usual with fighting men, such as theft or fights breaking out due to a misunderstanding in customs, pranks, or language. During the Crusades, the Assassins had stayed neutral and had not fought with Saladin against Christians. The Assassins were friendly with the Knights Templar and protected them in times of trouble. The leadership of the prince and the friendly relationship with the Knights Templar had led to an acceptance of our desert brothers.

Later in the day, as the prince was observing the practice with the Assassins, Ravenaire came up to him as if to ask him something. There was some animated conversation, when suddenly, Ravenaire used one of the Assassin moves and threw the prince down onto the sand. She pointed at him and laughed as he struggled to get up. There were some feints and jabs between the two, but then the prince picked her up and ran to the sea a short distance away. She kicked and squealed as he carried her. He then unceremoniously dropped her into the onrushing waves while laughing. He turned to walk away, when she lunged for him and drove him underwater. We all stopped our practice to watch the antics of the prince and Ravenaire. There was much splashing and laughing between the two. We all applauded the prince, who had a big smile on his face as Ravenaire waved to us. Finally, the prince picked her up and carried her to his tent. I enjoyed the playfulness between the prince and Ravenaire, as did the others.

We were on the move the next morning. The Dark Prince felt we had overstayed our visit. The prince was able to purchase horses for our travels.

He had French-speaking knights make individual purchases of horses as we traveled. It was a slow process to purchase a hundred horses without drawing attention. The knights purchasing the horses traveled alone and then met up with us with the horses they purchased. The animals were not warhorses but the high-spirited horses the French Basques were known for. The horses made for easier travel. A knight on foot was a sorry sight to watch.

We were watchful and had some of the Assassins on point. Brother Danner rode near the prince. Sir Arturo and the mighty Sir Baldassare were on either side of the prince and Ravenaire. I was farther back, protecting the rear with a handful of knights. The day promised to have good weather. The sky was blue, with little cloud cover. The afternoon would be hot.

We began to see local people on the road, mostly farmers going to market. There were some travelers but no soldiers. Some in the small crowds gave us suspicious looks and pointed at us. We did not wish to meet the French patrols.

It was noon, and the prince decided to have us avoid towns. It was cooler in the forests than on the roads, and we felt safer.

Around midday, I happened to look back to speak with one of the knights and catch some movement farther back in the forest. I spoke as softly as I could to Sir Borris. "Look ye back among the trees, and you will see we are being followed. Do not look now but in a little while. I do not want them to know we have seen them. Calmly spread the word to the other knights with us, so we do not alert those who follow us."

"Yes, my lord, I will spread the word quietly," Sir Borris replied in his usual gruff voice. "My lord Tristan, this ride through the countryside is all well and good, but I am a knight and would like nothing better than to bash and skewer someone! I am bored."

"Sir Borris, I will ride forward to alert the others. Do not provoke whoever is following us. I shall return shortly."

I urged my horse forward in an unhurried manner and spoke with Sir Arturo, Sir Baldassare, and the prince. We made as if we were having a good joke.

Sir Arturo said, "We are being followed? Ha! What fun!"

Sir Baldassare replied, "I do not see the fun in this. Ha ha."

The Dark Prince said, "My men need some fun. Let us engage these fellows and have some sport." He slapped Sir Arturo on the back and smiled.

Ravenaire said, "My lord, let us wait and see what happens. We are one hundred twenty strong. They will not risk trifling with us."

Sir Arturo said, "Ravenaire speaks truth. Let us wait and see. Ha ha."

The prince said, "I am in agreement with Ravenaire's counsel. We will wait. What fun this is."

We all laughed and carried on as if we did not know we were being followed. Slowly, the word was passed to the others, with the men appearing to be relaxed and joking among themselves. It was funny to watch the puzzled looks of the Assassins, who did not understand any of it until Tamir spoke to one of them and the word spread among them. Then they too laughed and patted one another on the back as they loosened their hidden daggers from their sheaths.

We continued on in that manner, with the men calm and self-assured, until we made camp in the evening. Tamir spoke with the Assassins. In a little while, a few of the Assassins melded into the darkness as the rest of us settled in around the campfires to eat and drink. We all were alert but tried to appear relaxed to anyone watching us.

Brother Danner approached me and said, "Brother Tristan, you had better sit, as you are a foot or so taller than most of us and make a good target."

I laughed and replied, "My lord, in my twenty years, I have been blessed. Our God will not forsake us."

Brother Danner laughed and motioned for me to sit. I joined him on the ground and looked to him for more conversation.

"Brother Tristan, we have history together. I worry about this adventure of the Dark Prince." Brother Danner motioned me closer as he continued.

"I am linked to the prince since the Battle of Naples. Our souls are linked. God spoke to me. He told me to protect the prince and help him to believe in God again. If I do not make this happen, it will cause a tragedy. I confide in you. No one else knows of this. Keep it that way."

I looked at Brother Danner in awe. I felt that he was blessed and that because we were both Templar knights, we had a special fellowship. We both had survived many battles, and God had always protected us.

I replied, "My lord Danner, you have my sword arm. What can I do?"

"Nothing for now. But keep close. I have a feeling I will be of need, and you more than any of the others will be able to help."

I nodded and smiled, feeling honored that Brother Danner had confided in me and had such trust. "I will not let you down. I make this pledge to you as a Templar knight and as a man."

Brother Danner smiled at me. He motioned for a servant to fill our cups with fresh wine and said, "I remember the good times when I was young. My father, Sir Simon du Montfort—vicar-general of Charles of Anjou, king of Sicily and youngest son of King Louis VIII of France— and my mother, Lady Margherita Aldobrandesca of Sovana, would have much laughter in our court. They were good times. Life was so carefree back then. It is good to have both Italian and French blood—great food, wine, and passion of life. I learned much from my father. He was a brilliant tactician and a leader of men. The soldiers revered my father and would do any command given. I was sent to my uncle Guy du Montfort to be a squire. Simon taught me this: *'Deo duce, ferro comitante, Deo adjuvante non timendum,'* which means 'With God as my leader and my sword as my companion, nothing should be feared.'

"Both my father, Simon, and his brother Guy received many medals and gifts from kings they served. Both brothers are wealthy land barons with many titles and land holdings in England, France, and Italy. As for me, after five years and hard work, I became a knight. There was a great ceremony with hundreds of people and great feasting that lasted for five days!"

Brother Danner smiled as he looked into the campfire, thinking of the old days. I enjoyed watching him. For now, he was not the strong, fierce knight who slayed dragons and had fought one hundred Saracens single-handedly. He was a man dreaming of the good times he had had as a little boy with his family. I let him be with his memories as I focused on the crackling fire.

After a time, Brother Danner turned to me and said, "What say you?" He was still smiling from his memories. "Tell me about your good times."

I smiled at both his tale and the youthful urgings that showed a tender side of this ferocious warrior. I looked once more to my fellow Templar, who was still smiling and encouraging me with his hand. I said, "I am the son of King Meliodas of Lyonesse and Queen Isabelle. The kingdom is surrounded by the sea. I can still remember the sounds of the great sea crashing upon the rocky cliffs and shoreline of my home. I could look out my bedroom windows and see nothing but the roiling ocean waves. Ha, I could even see sea monsters and dragons where the sea ends at the edge of the world. My mother, Queen Isabelle, would walk with me on the shore, and she would pick up pretty-colored shells to make necklaces for me. I wore them proudly. I would go fishing with one of the fishing folks, accompanied by one of my father's knights, and catch big fish that would almost pull me under. In fact, a few of those knights saved me from being pulled under by a big fish on more than one occasion. The knight would put to the sword the fish, in order for us not to sink in our boat with its thrashings.

"I was a squire to my uncle Mark, king of Cornwall, at Tintagel Castle. I was big for my age and was hard put by some of the knights of Cornwall, as they thought me older. As time went on, my body became hard with strong muscle, and I could hold my own with any of the knights. By sixteen, I was knighted by King Mark and was a trusted adviser. Knights of the castle became jealous of me and would challenge me in combat. I would smite these knights and beat them down in single combat. I eventually had most of the knights' grudging respect. My uncle had a saying that I have adopted: '*Aut viam inveniam aut faciam*,' which means 'Either to conquer or to die.'" I smiled at the memory as I looked into the fire.

Brother Danner said, "You are still big for your age!"

We both laughed. We were relaxed and enjoying our conversation. Good food was served to us, along with good wine to wash it down. It was a comfortable night, and the campfires and conversations of knights drifting through the camp helped us feel secure in that land.

CHAPTER 9

TRANSFORMATION

There was a commotion in camp, not far from where we sat. Brother Danner and I stood with our hands on our sword hilts. Three Assassins brought two strangers into the camp. The strangers appeared to be men handy with the sword. They both carried scars of battles and seemed to be at ease in an armed camp of warriors they did not know. The men projected an air of confidence. The prince and Tamir were summoned. They arrived almost immediately.

The prince motioned for the men to sit before him, with Tamir by his side. Everyone was curious about what was happening and pressed closer to hear what was said. Brother Danner and I moved closer to the prince to protect him if there was trouble.

The prince spoke. "Who are you, and what do you want?"

One of the men answered in a language we did not understand. Seeing our confusion, he began to speak French. "My name is Nico. I am Basque, and you are on my land. I ask you: What do you want, and why are you here?"

The prince laughed, considering we were 250 strong warriors, while this man was accompanied by only one. The prince replied, "I am a man in search of another, and these are my men. The man we seek is called Greco. He killed my father and his brothers in a cowardly attack with Serbian mercenaries. He also stole a wagon filled with gold that was to be a ransom for my father and his brothers. I want to punish Greco for what he did and to return the gold to its rightful place. Will you help me?"

Nico rubbed his dark beard. I could see clearly the long scar on the right side of his face, which ran from below his eye to his jaw. The crisscrossed scars on his wrists and forearms told me he was a seasoned warrior. Nico turned to his companion, and the two men had an intense conversation. There appeared to be a conflict between them.

Nico scratched his beard and told our prince, "Santos says you must be an important man to have all these men with you. He wants to know if there is a reward for us."

The prince smiled and said, "I would pay you a reward you both would be happy with."

Nico spoke to the man named Santos, and they again had an animated conversation. This time, they nodded in agreement. Nico said, "What does this man look like?"

The prince replied, "He is a big man with dark features."

Santos interrupted our prince, saying, "That describes half the men I know. What else?"

The prince continued, smiling. "This man Greco is ugly, with a scar on the left side of his face, from the forehead to the jaw." The prince brought a hand down the left side of his face. "He also has only half his right ear; the other half was bitten off in a fight. His nose has been broken a dozen times and has no real shape. He carries a shiny hatchet by his side so big." The prince spread his hands to show a blade size of a foot or so.

Santos looked down and said nothing. Nico also avoided eye contact and scratched his beard. Both became quiet. The prince glanced quickly around at his people and saw us nodding in agreement. Some of our men began to murmur among themselves. One said, "Make them talk. They know something."

The prince spoke in a commanding voice. "Where is Greco?"

Nico replied, "Let me ask my people and return in three days' time for an answer."

The prince, unsmiling, said in a deadly voice, "You will answer my question now, or by my dagger, you will not leave here and will be forgotten men with your bones picked clean by foul creatures."

Nico looked sullen, and Santos's eyes glanced about, looking for a way to escape. Quickly, they realized they would have to answer to the prince, for we were moving to surround them. Santos looked up at the prince and asked, "Where is my reward?"

The prince replied, "If I do not hear where Greco is hiding, my sword point will be your reward!"

Santos said, "It is not a fair thing you ask for. You hide behind all these warriors to protect you."

We all knew where this was going. I spoke out quickly. "Lord, let me have the honor to teach this cur respect to his betters!" I had my sword half out of its scabbard as I moved forward.

The mighty Sir Baldassare moved in front of me, saying, "No, my lord. Let me. I am bored and need a little exercise."

Brother Danner moved quickly and stood in front of Santos with sword drawn before anyone else. The amethysts on his sword hilt flashed a brilliant purple in the campfire light. "Fall on your knees, and beg forgiveness from our prince, or I will send your soul to hell!"

Santos cowered before Brother Danner and dropped to his knees. We were surprised by Brother Danner's quickness and the intensity he was showing. Santos said, "I see it takes all these warriors to protect this one man." He spread his arms out and continued. "I wonder how brave he truly is. Is he a sick man, an invalid? Or maybe he is not in his right mind. I think him to be a coward who has money and pays people to fight for him." Looking at the prince, he asked, "What say you?"

The prince moved closer. His face showed the fury he was trying to control. Brother Danner held his sword inches from Santos's neck, ready at any moment to thrust the blade home. The prince slowly looked around to see the mighty Sir Baldassare standing nearby with sword drawn. He next saw me beside Sir Baldassare, also with sword drawn, and his smile turned into a big grin. Sir Arturo stood next to the prince with his sword drawn, ready to shield the prince if there was trouble. I looked for Ravenaire and found her just behind the big bulk of Sir Baldassare, with a throwing dagger in her hand. She had a deadly look in her eyes that reminded me of a hunting falcon I once had had.

The prince turned his gaze to Santos and said, "I do not need any of these knights to take care of the vermin I see before me. You will be child's play for me. Stand up, and defend yourself. No one will interfere. I give you my word."

I saw a cunning grin that vanished in an instant as Santos stood. He looked around, saw us still standing within killing distance, and said, "You do not leave me much room to defend myself."

The prince was annoyed and told everyone to step back twenty paces to give room, using his hands to motion us back. He had not drawn his sword. The prince was thinking of fair play and not really looking at Santos. Santos had drawn his sword already, and he swung it at the prince. Everyone let out a loud gasp as the sword hissed through the air to strike the prince.

*

In that moment, fact and fiction merged into one. Some swore a transformation took place before their eyes. Others swore it was a miracle. I was undecided because it all happened too fast.

The Assassins claimed the devil came up from the ground in a whirlwind and struck Santos down. They always had felt the prince was supernatural when holding a sword. Arturo and the mighty Baldassare both stood rooted to the ground with their mouths open in surprise. Ravenaire had tears streaming down her cheeks.

Brother Danner and I would discuss the event for years afterward without coming up with an adequate explanation as to what truly had happened. Was it something in the campfire? Or had something fallen into the fire, such as a pine cone? All 250 warriors had an opinion as to whether it was a transformation or a miracle that happened that day, and they argued for hours, convinced of their positions. I left it in God's hands. Regardless, we all fell to our knees in awe and bowed to our prince.

It was late at night in the wilderness. The men were resting by the fires of our camp. The Dark Prince was speaking to Nico the Basque about himself. Arturo, Baldassare, Danner, Ravenaire, several knights, Tamir, and I were listening.

We were still in awe of the Dark Prince in his dealing with the treacherous Santos. The brilliant flash of light and the explosive burst of fire had surprised us. We had been blinded momentarily. We had seen the prince strike down Santos with his sword, left-handed, through the flickering light. We all knew that left-handedness was evil. The campfire flickered as shadows danced and played games around us.

Nico showed fear in being so near the Dark Prince of Naples. He thought the prince was the devil incarnate. But Nico still pledged fifty Basque fighters and maybe more. The Basques resented soldiers from other parts of France in their realm. They had held their own territory for a thousand years. Even the mighty Roman army could not defeat the Basques. The Moors could not defeat the Basques. The Basques were the best fighters in those parts. Nico understood why we were there—revenge for the deaths of the Dark Prince's family. The Basques would fight for a man seeking righteous revenge for his family, for family was most important.

As we added more logs to the fire, our party found comfort in its warmth and the filling meal and wine. We were all in good spirits. Stories were told, and the men laughed.

Nico began to tell us a tale in his peculiar accent. "The sounds of thunder and the clash of men fighting faded in the distance. The ground was slippery on the bare feet. I wanted to think it was just the storm that made the feet slip and not the blood and gore that made it so.

"The forest into which I ran was hushed and ominous. There was a foreboding that made me feel chilled with fear. I stopped running. My heart was beating so loudly I felt that all manner of creatures hidden in that dark place could hear it. The soft sound of the rain filtering through the trees was the first sound I heard, soon followed by the breath of a breeze carrying a sweet balsam smell. I was alone in a forest that stretched for hundreds of miles in all directions.

"I cautiously moved forward in the fading light, hoping to find a sheltered place. The wounds I had received began to throb more than before. I was weak and tired. I pushed myself forward, trying not to make any noise or trip and fall. Behind me, I heard the soft tread of a pursuer. The hunter had become the hunted. The warrior in me was now the prey. Was it a man or animal? I did not know. I tried to hurry, but it was no good. I was too weak from injuries and blood loss to continue.

"The misty rain felt cool on my skin. The sweet fragrance of the pine trees wafted through the air. It was darker now, and I could barely see. I was very tired, and my eyelids grew heavy. My legs betrayed me, and I slid to the forest floor.

"I felt my spirit grow restless for release. My eyelids fluttered open for a second, and before me stood my pursuer. We acknowledged each other silently, and I waited. I noticed the rain had stopped. My knife was no longer in my hand. Before me, a face loomed out of the mists of my eyes. He squatted in front of me. This man had a firm mouth, a strong and noble nose, and strange, symbolic scars marking both his cheeks. The symbolic scars did not take away the cruel beauty of his face. His eyes were an icy blue. Such eyes I had never seen before. His eyes were piercing and could see to my very soul. I saw his eyes narrow as he studied me, for they were all-knowing. He was wearing a blue beaded necklace that glowed and seemed to have a life of its own. On his right arm was a large metal armband with a strange design. Looped earrings of gold dangled from his ears. The man had long, thick hair the color of the sun. I had never seen such hair. I figured I must have been fading in and out of consciousness; nothing made any sense to me.

"I felt his hands on me, and then there was blackness. I was now somewhere else. It was peaceful. I was in no pain. The sweet smell of the pine trees engulfed me. I was one with the forest. Floating through the woods, I saw the wolves sunning themselves in a high meadow. I drifted among the trees and saw a great bear digging up roots to eat. To the west, a group of men were by a fire. I drifted by them, but they did not see me. One of the hunters glanced around and rubbed his arms as if they were cold.

"The sun shone on my face as I awakened. I felt the heat, and my eyes squinted from the sun's light. I moved without pain. I felt reborn. I tried to remember what had happened the night before. Was it a dream? I felt for the wounds I had, but there were none. I was puzzled. I leaped to my feet to journey from whence I had come. I caught a glint of sunlight reflecting off something on the forest floor. I bent down and picked up a looped earring and studied it. It looked familiar. Then I remembered. I had been visited by Basa-Jaun, the lord of the forest! He had healed me. I said my thanks to him and promised to sacrifice a lamb to him. I put the earring in the pouch hanging from my belt, next to my knife, and trotted back through the forest on a deer path, heading home. It was good to be alive. I still carry it. You want to see it?" Nico showed us the earring, and we all marveled at it. We could not identify the metal. Nico asked softly, "Dark Prince, are you cousins with Basa-Jaun?"

The Dark Prince merely smiled at him.

All the warriors in camp were enthralled by his story. I saw many smiles, including from Danner, Tamir the Assassin, Dana DeFusco, Arturo, Baldassare, and Ravenaire. Being a Templar knight, I had misgivings about the tale, as I knew there was only one God, not many gods, as the pagan believed.

CHAPTER 10

SCIPIO

Scipio had traveled a long way. He was tired and found a small, quiet stream to drink from and rest beside. Around him was thick forest. He cupped his hands and drank deeply as his sharp eyes scanned the forest. He listened for any foreign noise that did not belong to the forest. He did not see or hear anything unusual. Scipio relaxed and pulled a hunk of cheese, dried meat, and a small chunk of bread from his pack. After a time, he stretched out on the forest floor and rested. His dagger and sword were within easy reach.

A young man of sixteen years, Scipio was on the tall side for his age. He was wiry, but his growing body promised to fill out and become muscle. Scipio was on the run. His mother had been attacked when she went to market while Scipio worked the farm. A neighbor going to market saw what looked like a bundle of clothes just off the path. He stopped his horse-drawn wagon and walked over to the bundle. He found Scipio's mother just off the path and saw her attackers running into the forest. He could do no more for the woman. He gently lifted her into his wagon and turned back to his neighbor's farm.

Scipio was grief-stricken. He tried not to cry in front of his neighbor, but alas, he could not stop the tears. A priest was summoned, and a burial was made on the farm, near the rosebushes she had loved. His neighbors gave their condolences and promised to look after the farm after Scipio made a solemn vow to avenge his mother's death. He took the sword his father had given him and packed bread, cheese, and dried meat. He told everyone he was going to track down the killers and would return. The people present all wished him well and good hunting.

Two days later, he found the killers of his mother at a small camp up in the hills. The three were by a fire, tending to their late meal of the day. They had no idea they were being tracked. Scipio's father had taught him well. His father was in Rome, a general in the army. The city-states of Italy were petty dukedoms of the powerful. His father, Cornelius, was a brilliant tactician and soldier. He was the best general Rome had had in recent times.

Scipio entered the camp. The three men were surprised and quickly huddled together on the other side of the campfire. The leader, a tall, dark-featured man in his forties, spoke in a harsh voice. "Who are you? What do you want?"

Scipio responded, "I want revenge for the death of my mother."

The three men cautiously looked Scipio up and down and then laughed. They saw a tallish boy on the verge of manhood with curly black hair and dark eyes. The leader said, "Come back when you are all grown up. You are just a pup."

Scipio drew his dagger quickly and said as he threw it, "Justice will be done." The dagger struck the leader in his chest.

The leader was surprised and looked at the dagger. Blood welled up and spilled from the side of his mouth as a dark stain spread on his shirt front. He slowly fell to his knees. He was still looking at the dagger, not believing he was about to die. He tried to pull it out but was too weak from the blood loss. The man's spirit was soon given up.

The two other men panicked and started to run. Scipio leaped through the campfire with his sword drawn and cut down a second man. The third man turned to fight, but in minutes, Scipio killed him with a masterful backstroke. The fight had lasted about five minutes from start to finish.

Scipio went through the men's clothes and found his mother's purse and money. He also found other coins of the realm that the men had stolen. Scipio left the camp and headed back home. In two days, he arrived and met with his neighbors. He told them what had happened and where the camp was with the three dead thieves.

All was forgotten until eight days later, when the sheriff arrived with five men-at-arms to arrest him for killing the three men. Scipio tried to explain what had happened, but the sheriff was unmoved. It seemed one of the men had been a nephew of a wealthy nobleman, who was demanding the arrest. He had paid off the sheriff and wanted the name cleared.

"Self-defense is no reason to kill three men. You took their money! The courts are to decide the judgment," the sheriff said. "I arrest you for the killing. Take this man."

The men-at-arms moved forward to take Scipio. Scipio moved faster, throwing a bucket of milk he was taking into his home, hitting the lead man. The men were taken by surprise and collided with one another. Scipio ran into the house and grabbed his sword, dagger, and backpack. Never breaking stride, he dove through a window in a back room and headed for the forest.

Later in the day, Scipio ran to a neighbor and told the man what had happened. The man was surprised and promised he would try to help. The man's wife hurried to give Scipio some fresh bread, cheese, and dried meat to help him on his way.

At sixteen years of age, Scipio had much to live for. His father had high expectations of him to be an outstanding military leader. Scipio had shown his father brilliant military tactics already. The son had accompanied his father on a few of his battles and could read the battlefield immediately. It was uncanny how Scipio could anticipate the enemy's next move. Scipio had chosen to run the farm while his father was on campaign but planned to join him later in the year, after the harvest.

Scipio woke a few hours later to the sounds of hounds in the distance. Immediately, he gathered his sword and dagger, grabbed his pack, and disappeared into the forest. He knew he did not have much time before the hounds found him. A chill went through him as he thought about the dogs.

The hounds were fierce war dogs bred and used to tear apart any man they were tracking. Weighing more than two hundred pounds and standing more than a yard tall at the shoulder, they had no fear. Their masters could barely control them. The hounds had originated with the old Roman legions' mastiffs. Over the years, the great wolves of the north had added to the bloodlines, producing a more savage animal that not only was a great tracker but also had increased size, speed, and endurance. There was no escape from the hounds once they had a scent.

The handlers encouraged the hounds to eat their prey. It was cheaper and more convenient than packing extra food for them. Handler and hound could travel faster, and there was greater motivation for the hound to fill its two-hundred-pound body with food it brought down after the chase.

Scipio had to lose the hounds. He ran through the stream, trying not to trip and injure himself. He slowed down from the initial panic of running all out. His full sprint lasted for less than ten minutes before he became winded. After he caught his breath and his heart stopped banging against his ribs in protest, he slowed down. The rocks were uneven and slippery as he ran through the stream. The stream had chest-high pools, which slowed him. Scipio had no idea where the stream would lead but felt if he continued to travel downward, it would lead to a river.

It seemed as if he had been slipping and sliding in the stream for hours. Scipio could hear a faint noise of rushing water in the distance. He felt relief that he was almost to safety. Suddenly, he heard splashing behind him. A chill went up his spine. He drew his dagger and turned. At the same time he turned, he was slammed off his feet by a huge black wolf with long, dagger-like, glistening teeth.

Scipio hit the water and went under as the devil hound tried to sink its teeth into him. He tried to keep his head above water and protect himself from the savage attack. He stabbed and thrust his dagger into the hound with one hand while protecting his face and throat with the other. The hound was in a frenzy, biting and shaking its huge head in its attack. Scipio realized the water was saving his life. The water was a buffer between him and those terrible teeth. However, he feared he might drown as the hound's feet held him under. The weight and the shifting legs of the hound pressed him down, doing more harm than the big teeth. Scipio felt the nails of the dog ripping him as he protected his face and neck. He knew he did not have much time to live.

As they were locked in a fight to the death, the current in the stream moved them forward. Sometimes Scipio had his head above water, but most of the time, the hound did. The water began to move faster as they tumbled over each other.

On a bank above them, three men and three hounds watched the struggle between the boy and their fastest hound. One of the men drew an arrow on his bow and let it fly. The archer smiled as the arrow found its mark as boy and hound tumbled over the thunderous hundred-foot falls. The archer said to the other men in an angry voice, "I lost a good hound. He was the best."

One of the other men mumbled, "It looks like we lost the boy. There will be no reward for him, dead or alive. No one could survive that fall."

The archer replied, "My hound was chewing him up as they went over. I do not think the boy will survive both the hound and the falls. Our work is done."

The three men put leashes on the remaining hounds; the lashings to close their mouths were intact. The men were disappointed they had not captured the fugitive. They had wanted to have some sport with the boy and the hounds. It was difficult to train the hounds, and one could never fully trust them. The hounds were wild creatures and would sometimes attack their handlers. The men and hounds headed back from whence they had come.

*

After Scipio pulled the arrow out of his thigh, he wrapped his thigh with a cloth strip torn from his shirt to help stop the bleeding. He then lay down by the riverbank for a time, trying to gather his wits as to all that had just happened. He had thought he was being careful by using the streams for travel to cut his scent from pursuing hounds.

Despite all his efforts, Scipio had been tracked and attacked by one of the vicious hounds from hell, which he had fought to the death, and he had fallen over a waterfall 150 feet high. He then had been plunged underwater by the waterfall and struggled to the surface. He had been swept downstream by the powerful river, bouncing off rocks and fighting off debris, such as fallen trees. It was a rough way to end a day. Scipio was exhausted and lay where he was, too tired to look for shelter for the night. *Tomorrow*, he thought, *will be a new day to plan*, and he fell into a deep, troubled sleep.

The next morning, Scipio woke up and was startled and then terrified to see the hound from hell curled up beside him. Cold sweat sprang from his forehead, and a chill went immediately up his spine. Too petrified to move a muscle, Scipio moved only his eyes to quickly scan the area for a knife or sword. He did not know when or how the hound had found him or why the hound had not torn him apart while he slept.

Scipio tentatively moved slowly from where he lay to try to put space between himself and the hound. The hound did not stir, which surprised Scipio. Scipio looked quickly around for his dagger and sword. Upon locating his weapons, he rushed to grab them. Then, turning quickly with sword in hand, he looked for the hound. The hound did not stir and continued to lie on its side. The rise and fall of the hound's side showed it was alive. Scipio wondered why it did not attack.

Carefully moving closer, Scipio studied the hound. It looked like a huge black wolf. Its mouth was open, and its red tongue hung out as it panted. Scipio saw the three-inch double-fanged teeth on both sides of its jaws and shuddered. Looking closer, he saw bloody patches on the beast's side. Some of the wounds still oozed blood, while the others were crusted and matted. Scipio listened more closely and noticed the breathing of the beast seemed to be ragged and irregular.

Indecision was in Scipio's mind. When he heard the soft whine of the beast, it gave him pause. Startled, he looked to the beast. Their eyes locked, and Scipio saw deep intelligence and pain in the beast. The wolf saw an equal. The adrenaline rush of fight-or-flee evaporated from Scipio. He suddenly felt compassion and wanted to help the beast. Scipio bent down, ripping strips of cloth from his shirt, and began to dress the wounds. The beast closed its eyes and allowed Scipio to comfort it.

Scipio fashioned a bucket to carry water from the river to the hound. Made from vines, leaves, mud, and other vegetation, the bucket lost about half its contents on each trip. The hound and Scipio did not seem to mind as they developed a friendship and were eager for each other's company. Scipio set up snares to catch rabbits and other small creatures of the forest and shared the meat with the hound. The hound preferred raw meat, while Scipio cooked his meat over a campfire. The hound gained strength and improved each day under Scipio's care.

As time went on, the hound would try to eat Scipio's meals, which resulted in friendly wrestling matches at Scipio's expense. The hound was always gentle with him, but in their play, Scipio could feel the massive strength of the hound and was awed by its quickness. The hound would pin Scipio down and then lick his face until Scipio cried out, laughing, "Enough! Get off me, you big oaf!" The hound could tell by Scipio's voice that he had had enough and would let him up. As soon as Scipio was standing, the hound would use its speed to race around Scipio. Using its muscular shoulders, it would bump Scipio behind his knees and knock him down again. The hound thought it was great fun and would sit with a big, wolfish smile on its face, watching Scipio. Scipio, bruised and sore, would dust himself off and give the hound a look that showed he did not appreciate the trick.

One day the hound entered the forest on its own and was gone for a few hours. Scipio was worried the hound was gone forever and wondered if it had returned to its original master or returned to the wild and joined a wolf pack. Later in the day, the hound returned with an adult stag in its jaws. The hound dropped the two-hundred-pound stag at Scipio's feet and then sat there with tail wagging. Scipio was astonished that the hound had returned and had felt good enough to hunt. The hound had fought a stag, killed it, and brought it back to share, which humbled Scipio. They would eat well for the next several days. Scipio praised the hound, petting, hugging, and making a big fuss. The gentle manner and kind words of Scipio from the time the hound had found him wounded by the riverbank gave the hound a new sense of purpose and absolute devotion to his new master.

Scipio began skinning the stag. He worked meticulously with the deerskin, making sure he scraped all the fat off the skin and did not tear the hide. The task took him most of the afternoon. He then pegged out the hide to stretch it. He used his urine on the hide to preserve it. The hound saw what Scipio had done and, curious, went over to the hide. After sniffing the hide and finding the scent of its new friend, the hound wagged its tail and lifted its leg. A yellow stream splattered over the hide. The hound sniffed its work again, wagged its tail, and then joined Scipio.

Scipio made a fire using many freshly cut green branches from the maple and oak trees of the forest, which created much smoke. He then began to gut the deer. The hound claimed the innards while Scipio quartered the meat. He then rigged up a primitive spit. While sections of the meat were smoked and roasted, Scipio cut smaller pieces of meat and skewered them on sharp branches to place on the fire. He worked for the entire remaining day and the next two processing the meat.

The hound was constantly at his side, sniffing this and checking out that, giving its approval to its new partner. The hound enjoyed all the new things it saw its human doing. It would wag its tail and appeared to be smiling, shoving its nose or body into whatever Scipio was doing.

The hound was into every aspect of cooking the meat. The hound now had freedom it had never known before and was inquisitive as to what its human friend would do next. It was also treated with love and kindness by Scipio, not beaten with a club, whipped, or kept in a cage.

A bear! Scipio could not believe his eyes. A bear had followed the scent of meat to their camp. It was big, hungry, and short-tempered. The bear lifted its nose high as it moved its massive head from side to side. Knocking the makeshift spit over when it found no meat, it gave an angry growl as it sent pieces of the wood spit flying into the air with one mighty swipe of its right paw. Sniffing the air, the mighty bear stood up.

Eleven towering feet of hunger and muscle, the bear located the meat hanging from a limb of a big oak tree. Scipio pulled his sword and dagger from his belt and ran to stand in front of the tree that held the meat. The bear saw Scipio for the first time and went into a rage. The bear advanced, ripping small bushes from the ground into the air. Scipio could see froth streaming from the bear's mouth as it advanced. Scipio went into a crouch, holding the sword and dagger in front of him.

The bear moved to within twenty feet of Scipio, stood up on its hind legs, and roared. The bear snapped its teeth as it looked down at Scipio. Scipio thought, *This is the end*. The great bear lowered itself onto all four legs and slowly advanced. Scipio knew he was helpless against such an animal, but it was too late to run. He was making his last stand against the beast and hoped the gods would look kindly down at him.

From the left of Scipio came a black blur. The hound attacked the huge bear from the rear, grabbing the right rear leg with its powerful jaws and ripping into the bear's hamstring. The bear roared out in pain. The hound used its massive shoulders and jaws, shaking the leg and inflicting much damage to the already torn muscles of the bear's leg. The bear made another swipe at the hound, catching it on the left side and sending the hound through the air and away from the bear's badly damaged leg. The bear struggled to stand, but the damaged leg gave out and could not support the bear's weight. The hound slowly stood. Its left side showed the bloody claw marks the bear had inflicted.

Bear and hound faced off with each other. The hound, with its formidable teeth showing in a snarl, advanced slowly. The bear could only squat, facing the slow advance of the hound, waiting for the hound to come in range of its strong arms and deadly claws. With a flash of movement, the hound leaped upon the bear and bit deeply into the back of its neck. The double fangs of the hound severed the big vein of lifeblood. The bear gave out a bellow of rage as it tried to shake the hound off its back. A powerful swipe of the bear's claws knocked the hound off its back and within a few feet of the bear.

The bear struggled to crawl to where the big hound lay. The loss of blood made the bear weak. With one mighty whack of its big paw, the sharp claws dug into the hound, inflicting grievous injury. The hound just lay there next to the bear, barely breathing, as blood poured from the open wounds. Some of the hound's fur was ripped back, exposing some of its ribs. Flies slowly started buzzing around both animals as they lay there not moving. Scipio moved cautiously toward the hound. Upon closer examination, he saw the bear was dead. Scipio lifted the hound's head into his lap and spoke softly while gently stroking his friend. After a time, the hound feebly wagged its tail and looked at Scipio with pain-clouded eyes.

A man in black slowly emerged from the forest and came silently up to Scipio. Scipio was startled when the man said, "Is this your animal?"

Scipio immediately laid the dog's head gently on the ground and whirled to his feet with sword drawn, facing the stranger.

The stranger laughed and calmly said, "Boy, put down your sword. I do not wish to kill you."

Scipio studied the strange man in black for a long moment and then lowered his sword. Scipio noticed the man spoke with a strange dialect, and his manner suggested he was from the Middle East. Scipio's father had told him of deadly men called the Assassins, who always dressed in black, with their faces covered so only their eyes showed. They dressed like that when they were hired to kill.

The man in black had an air of confidence in his speech and manner that spoke volumes. It was clear he could have killed Scipio on a whim. The strange man bent down on one knee to examine the hound. After a few moments, he asked, "What name is this beast called?"

Scipio felt embarrassed and said, "I have not named it."

The man in black shook his head slowly and said, "The beast has shown much courage. It should have a name!"

Scipio knelt beside the man in black and asked, "Will it live?"

The man in black said, "I am called Hassan. What name do they call you?"

"I am called Scipio."

Hassan nodded. As Hassan looked over the hound, he told Scipio the things he needed to help the hound. Scipio went into the woods to gather herbs, certain vines, moss, and the bark of a pine tree. Hassan then had Scipio start a fire to boil water. Hassan cut out the stomach bladder from the great bear and squeezed out its contents. He then filled the stomach bladder with water from a nearby stream and tied off both ends with cord. He placed the stomach bladder near hot coals, so as not to put holes in it and lose the hot water. When they could hear that the water boiled, Hassan said, "We are ready to start. Tie the muzzle of the beast with the vines so it cannot open its mouth to bite."

It took several days for the hound to sit up and walk. By that time, Hassan and Scipio were becoming friends. They had skinned the bear and had fires going to smoke the meat to preserve it. During their time together, Hassan learned that Scipio was only sixteen years old, and he taught Scipio to be a better swordsman. They practiced for hours. During their secessions, Scipio learned new moves and defenses. The hound had accepted Hassan, and the three of them enjoyed their time together. Eventually, Hassan told Scipio he would have to report to his master within the next two days. Scipio felt bad about losing his friend so soon.

At the end of the second day, after their usual lesson, Scipio asked Hassan, "Could I come with you to your master? I have no other place to go and could be useful to your master."

Hassan had grown to like the boy. In some ways, the boy reminded him of when he had been younger and life had been simple. "Many of us may not live when this mission is done. I want you to understand this before we continue with this conversation."

The boy nodded that he understood.

Hassan continued. "We are one hundred twenty warriors strong. If the French find us, it will be a fight to the death. There will be no quarter given. My prince is after a very dangerous man who killed his father and all his relatives and then stole a ransom of gold, silver, and jewels. Friends of my prince have told us this man called Greco has a small army to protect him. Greco is the man we want to hand over to my prince." Hassan leaned closer. "Scipio, the chance that we will run into the French is high. After that, who knows who will survive? Then those of us left will continue until we find Greco and fight his dangerous men, men who have no honor. This adventure could cost you your young life."

Scipio answered, "My friend, as you know, I am a good fighter and can stand against everyone but you. I have courage. I stood up to the bear until the hound fought and killed it. I am trustworthy. And besides, I have no place to go."

Hassan replied, "I will bring you to my prince, and he will decide if you are to come with us. But first, we must give your wolf a name. Do you have any ideas?"

Scipio thought for a time and then said, "Wolf."

Hassan laughed and said, "The beast deserves better than that. How about the Black Death, Night Hunter, Shadow Dancer, or Night Hawk?"

Scipio gave long thought to Hassan's names, tossing them over in his mind. The hound came up behind Scipio and knocked him down in a playful manner. Scipio tried to stand, but the hound pinned him down and thoroughly licked his face. Scipio called out, "Back, Black Death!" but the hound continued and harried Scipio, knocking him to the ground again.

Hassan stepped back and laughed at the antics between the two.

Scipio tried again. "Down, Night Hunter!" he said, but the hound continued to trip Scipio and, using its powerful body, knocked Scipio to the ground once again. Scipio was losing his patience and said, "Shadow Dancer, sit!" The hound playfully grabbed Scipio's arm and dragged him down to the ground.

Hassan was beside himself with laughter at their antics, enjoying himself at the expense of Scipio.

Desperately, Scipio said, "If you do not want me to beat you with a big, ugly stick, I command you, Night Hawk, to sit."

To the amazement of Scipio and Hassan, the hound obeyed and sat. The hound accepted the name Night Hawk.

Scipio looked at Hassan and said, "Who would have thought a name could be so much trouble?"

Hassan smiled and said, "A name is everything. It tells the world who you are. It gives your history to people. Your name tells where you come from, what your politics are, and what god you pray to. This could be a good thing or not so good. Your name will either be agreeable or disagreeable to others. It could be the difference between life and death."

For much of that day and the next, Scipio worked with Night Hawk, teaching him commands over and over until the hound became proficient. Hassan was impressed with the beast's learning abilities and the teamwork between the boy and the beast. They were a formidable team. The boy, at sixteen years, was a good swordsman. Scipio and Hassan fashioned a leather leash and collar for Night Hawk to keep him close and under control when needed.

Hassan left early in the morning, saying he would return later that day. Meanwhile, Scipio continued to work with Night Hawk.

When Hassan came back, he brought two pack horses to transport all their meat. Hassan said they had to go to the west when they left, so as not to have a run-in with an angry farmer. The horses were shy with Night Hawk. It took some time for Night Hawk to behave and for the horses to settle. The men worked on lashing long poles together for the horses to pull after the meat was loaded. Hassan showed Scipio how to lash the poles with vines to hold the meat on the poles.

Hassan also showed Scipio how to make saddlebags for Night Hawk to carry meat. Night Hawk thought it was great fun to tear apart the saddlebags, but after many reprimands and saddlebags, Night Hawk finally got the idea. He had a proud gait while carrying his share of the load. Night Hawk was carrying 150 pounds of meat.

Later in the day, Hassan took the lead, and both men walked their animals loaded with meat and headed west. They would travel for two days and nights, avoiding villages and people. During that time, the men and Night Hawk formed a bond.

CHAPTER 11

THE DARK PRINCE MEETS THE BIG, BAD WOLF

When they were within a few miles of the outside perimeter of Assassins, Hassan said to Scipio, "Remember, you are meeting royalty. He is the prince of Naples. You will give him every courtesy, and you will protect him at all costs. Whatever he asks of you, you will do it immediately. Understood?"

Scipio looked into Hassan's eyes and said in a nervous voice, "I understand. I will do everything you ask."

"And another thing. You will keep Night Hawk on a tight leash and have his muzzle bound when we meet the outer perimeter of guards and even into the camp," said Hassan. "I do not want any undo deaths to occur, including that of your beast."

"I will also do this," responded Scipio. "I have grown much attached to Night Hawk. I do not want to see him harm the prince or any of his men, nor do I want him to be injured."

Night Hawk gave forth a deep growl and leaped forward, pulling Scipio after him. The hound pulled loose and continued his charge into the forest. Soon there was much yelling, followed by the sounds of a fierce fight. Scipio and Hassan arrived in time to see an Assassin on the ground with Night Hawk on top of him. The hound was pinning the Assassin to the ground. The muzzle on the beast prevented a deadly accident. Scipio grabbed the leash and pulled Night Hawk off the man. The Assassin had a dagger drawn and was about to use it, when Hassan yelled out something in a foreign language that stopped him.

Hassan hurried to the Assassin and rapidly explained, pointing to Scipio and Night Hawk. The Assassin picked himself up from the ground and dusted himself off while muttering to himself. He angrily spoke to Hassan in a foreign language, pointing at the boy and his alert beast. Hassan replied in the same language but much calmer, and the Assassin disappeared back into the forest.

Scipio asked Hassan, "Where did that man go? I am sorry Night Hawk attacked him."

Hassan replied, "He is going back to the main camp to tell the others that we are coming in. He was angry that he had been found by the beast. We are lucky there is a muzzle on Night Hawk. You must keep him under better control when we enter the camp, or there will be terrible consequences."

Scipio, Hassan, and Night Hawk made their way through the forest, uphill and downhill, across a small stream, and then over a hill again. When they climbed up another hill, they saw firelight from a big camp. Many men moved in and out of the firelight. As they made their way to the camp on a hill to the east, Night Hawk started a low growl deep within his throat, alerting Scipio and Hassan that there were men nearby.

Scipio held Night Hawk's muzzle and whispered, "Quiet." Their eyes locked, and Night Hawk went silent but stayed alert.

A few moments later, several Assassins emerged from the darkness and greeted Hassan. They were introduced to Scipio, but their eyes went almost immediately to the beast. They had heard about the beast and were curious to see him. They marveled at his size and power but kept their distance. Mustafa, the Assassin who had been attacked by the beast, had not exaggerated the hound's size and strength. They were surprised at how the young man could keep the beast under control. The big black beast was twice the weight of Scipio, and his head was halfway up Scipio's chest. The beast would have been much taller than Scipio if it had stood up on hind legs, close to eight feet tall.

The Assassins led the way into camp, followed by Scipio, Night Hawk, and Hassan. As they approached the campfire, Scipio tightened the leash on Night Hawk and spoke to him in a calming voice. Soon they entered the camp. Those in the camp stopped what they were doing to see the new arrivals. As Scipio and Night Hawk made their way closer to the campfires, people gasped at the sight of the beast. Night Hawk behaved himself as they stood there while two warriors milled about looking at them and speaking in loud and soft tones like the waves of an ocean on the shore.

Food was unloaded from the horses and Night Hawk. The men were happy they were getting freshly smoked venison and bear meat. They marveled at the bearskin. Hassan explained that the beast had killed the bear while defending Scipio. Much talk was generated about the conflict of bear and beast. As the story made the rounds, it changed with every retelling.

The Dark Prince and Ravenaire came forward to greet the new arrivals. Danner, Arturo, Baldassare, and I accompanied them. Arturo and Baldassare moved next to the prince as added protection. Ravenaire was taken with the beast. She threw caution to the wind and approached him. The beast was calm and allowed Ravenaire to approach him. She spoke in a soft voice, as one would to a small child, and gently stroked his head. Ravenaire felt sorry that the beast had to be muzzled and reached down to loosen the muzzle. The black beast responded by pushing forward, dragging Scipio, and licking Ravenaire's hand. When the beast moved forward, everyone reached for a weapon to leap in and save Ravenaire. But when we saw the beast lick her hand and start acting like an overgrown puppy, we all relaxed and laughed at ourselves, marveling at how brave Ravenaire was. None of the two hundred warriors would have gone near the beast, never mind would have pet him.

Ravenaire played with the beast, who jumped around in a playful manner with her. Night Hawk was gentle, licking her face, rubbing against her, and making peculiar sounds. At one point, the beast lay down and let Ravenaire rub his belly. Everyone enjoyed the antics of the beast and the beautiful Ravenaire. Scipio had worried that something bad would happen and that the beast would be killed. Upon seeing Night Hawk and the princess play and enjoy themselves, he visibly relaxed.

Hassan came and stood by Scipio and then introduced him to the Dark Prince and Ravenaire.

The Dark Prince beckoned Scipio to come forward. The prince was smiling and in a good mood, watching the interplay of the beauty and the beast. "How did you come by such an animal?"

Scipio replied as he bowed his head in respect to the prince, "I was being pursued by men with their hounds. My mother was robbed and killed by bad men. I tracked the men and killed them. The local officials knew of the thieves but did nothing. By my actions in killing the men, the officials put a bounty on my head. Three bounty hunters with their hounds tracked me down. This one caught up with me in a stream and attacked me. We fought as the current swept us. I could barely breathe with the hound on top of me most of the time. I pulled my dagger and fought for my life.

"We were swept over a hundred-fifty-foot waterfall and carried downstream. I crawled out of the water and found an arrow in my leg. I broke the arrow shaft and pulled one part out of my leg. I pulled the shaft with the blade out the other side of my leg. I tore part of my shirt to wrap around the wound so it would stop bleeding. I must have passed out then. In the morning, the hound was sleeping next to me. He could have killed me. I do not know why he did not. I saw in his eyes intelligence and hurt. I nursed him back to health, and he has been with me from that time. The Assassin Hassan must have been watching from the forest for a few days before he showed himself to me. Hassan showed me how to use plants from the forest to help him heal. I have tried to work with my hound, and he is quick to learn. There are some things he already knows, but I do not know what, and it gives me worry."

The Dark Prince looked concerned and said, "That was quite a story. Why are you here?"

"I was told by Hassan that you are a good man and that you are looking for the man who killed your father. Much the same story as mine. You need men who can fight. I can fight. My hound, Night Hawk, will be very valuable. He can find the Assassins, no matter where they hide! If he can do that, he can find the bad man who killed your father."

The Dark Prince smiled at the boy. After a brief pause, he said, "This will be a very dangerous adventure. The French will not like me or my men, should they discover us. They will have patrols out that we will surely run into. Then there is the man Greco. He is the bad man I am hunting. Greco has a small army of mercenaries who are cutthroats and killers. It will be a dangerous adventure, and I will be concerned for your safety."

"Let me prove my skills to you. Pick any warrior here, and I will show you my skills."

The Dark Prince smiled and replied, "These warriors have spilled blood for me. They are the best there is. I hesitate to put you in harm's way to prove your skills. Arturo, I want to see if this boy can defend himself. Come here, and let us see what he knows. I do not want any blood spilled."

Scipio and Arturo gave each other a slight nod and touched swords. Everyone backed up to give them space. Night Hawk came instantly alert, transforming from a lap dog with Ravenaire to a protective, wild beast. With a deep, menacing growl, he slowly stepped forward, stiff-legged, until he came between Scipio and Arturo. Arturo's eyes immediately switched to the beast who stood in front of him with gleaming white teeth and glinting yellow eyes. Arturo slowly backstepped.

The black beast, with its hackles raised, slowly advanced. Scipio immediately put up his sword and grabbed the leash of Night Hawk.

Scipio gave a command to stop, and Night Hawk stopped but kept his eyes on Arturo. Scipio went to the dog and spoke to him, gently stroking the dog's head and back. Night Hawk visibly relaxed. There was a sudden hush in the camp. Everyone froze, afraid that any sound or sudden movement would trigger the beast into attacking Arturo.

The Dark Prince, after seeing Scipio calm the beast, coolly said, "Scipio, you have proven yourself this night. I have decided to have you assigned with the Assassins, who have Tamir as their leader. You will do whatever he asks of you. I feel you will be of great value there. Pull the black beast back. I want everyone, one at a time, to slowly come up to the beast. Let him get your scent."

Baldassare, Brother Danner, and I had drawn our swords while moving closer to protect Arturo, concerned Arturo would be torn apart by the beast. Now there were low mutterings and murmurs among the warriors about letting the beast near them.

When the prince heard the men complain, he said, "I will go first." He strode to where Scipio was petting and talking softly to Night Hawk and said, "Let the black beast get my scent. I want him to know all who are here, to have him recognize that we are friends and that all others are his enemy."

With that, he slowly put his hand out palm up to allow Night Hawk to freely sniff. Scipio held his breath as Night Hawk's huge head moved to the hand of the Dark Prince and got his scent. The prince slowly moved his hand and petted the beast. Night Hawk responded, looking relaxed and wagging his tail. Danner and I, the Templar knights, were next. Eventually, all the men went up to the beast. Night Hawk was alert in the beginning with the Dark Prince and the next ten people.

Scipio had to constantly stop Night Hawk from pulling, tugging, jumping up, and hitting someone with his big paws in a playful manner. When Ravenaire went through the line, the beast was beside himself with joy. Licking her face and nudging her to pet him, he made the same peculiar noises he had made earlier. They both seemed to be having great fun.

I was nearby and heard the conversation between Arturo and Baldassare.

Arturo said, "I was really concerned the beast would eat me. His yellow eyes seemed to light up. The fangs! To all the saints in heaven, I would rather face twenty armed Saracens than that beast!"

Baldassare replied, "I thought he would take an arm off and was wondering what the women in your life would say. Would you say you had been in a great battle with a dragon you slew, or would you say you fought a hundred fifty Saracens by yourself and received that mere battle wound?"

Arturo punched Baldassare lightly on the shoulder, saying, "The beast should have locked eyes on you. He would have been thinking, *So much meat. Where do I begin? Maybe Baldassare's fat head.*"

I said to the prince, "I almost stepped forward to thrust my sword into the beast to protect Arturo."

The Dark Prince said, "I am glad I stopped the exhibition between Arturo and the boy when I did. I had no idea the beast was so protective of the boy. This is a good thing. The beast has courage. I think he could have attacked Arturo but held back to see what was going to happen. If Arturo had continued, the beast would have attacked him. The wolf was saying, 'If you hurt Scipio, then you deal with me.' Putting the boy and the beast together with the Assassins is a good match. What say you, Tamir?"

Tamir had been talking with one of the Assassins who had just returned. Tamir walked five steps over to join the Dark Prince. When he was standing next to the prince, he responded, "The beast is a formidable weapon. Hassan has told me of a terrible fight the black wolf had with a brown cave bear. Hassan brought the bearskin. It stretches more than two tall men! I think the boy and wolf will complement my men. It will be a good match. Did you see the size of the double fangs on both sides of his mouth?"

*

"Uncle Tristan, how big was that wolf?" asked Franco.

"Were you really afraid of the beast?" asked Mark Anthony.

"Ravenaire was not afraid. I think women are braver than boys," said Rose Marie.

I laughed. "You know how brave Uncle Baldassare is. Well, you should have seen the look on his face when he saw the wolf! The wolf, standing on his hind legs, would have stood taller than I!"

CHAPTER 12

ON THE MARCH

The prince's new strategy was to have Scipio and the wolf work out front with a few of the Assassins as scouts, to find enemy patrols and decide whether to attack them and take no prisoners or stay unnoticed. I would work with them as a liaison to the prince and the Assassins.

Tamir said to Scipio, "I want you to go to the front with the black wolf. Stay hidden, and be very quiet. You will be the eyes and ears of our men. It is a big responsibility. Consider all men you see out there to be the enemy. You will use your discretion. If there are only a few men, let loose the wolf. Two Assassins will be with you to help you. If there are many, stay hidden. One of the Assassins will come back and let Sir Tristan know. Sir Tristan and the prince will make a decision as to whether we will engage or not. Keep the black wolf quiet, and both of you are to stay well hidden with the other Assassin. I will send the second Assassin to tell you what Sir Tristan and the prince decide. Of course, I will have a say in this matter also. Do you understand?"

Scipio responded, "I will do as you say. I am honored to do this. I will not let the men down."

Tamir said, "Go now, and search out what is before us. Keep about a mile in front of us. Be as quiet as you can with the beast. Do not let him bark or chase a small animal. You will keep the wolf on a leash at all times but no muzzle. I want the wolf to be able to use his great fangs. Is this understood?"

Scipio nodded and moved forward in front of the warriors. Hassan and another Assassin soon joined him. I took my position next to Tamir.

An hour later, the Dark Prince and his followers left the campsite in a loose formation, with the Assassins spread out on both flanks and some two hundred yards forward of the army.

Brother Danner and I rode near the Dark Prince, Ravenaire, and Tamir. It was a sunny day, with a few soft clouds. Arturo and the mighty Baldassare rode on either side of the prince.

Arturo said, "I am glad the black wolf is in front of us rather than behind—and I am mounted on a horse."

Baldassare gave a short laugh and said, "I think that black wolf likes you. I could see it in his yellow eyes. He had a hungry look. I suggest you ride forward and pet him. Or maybe give him a bone to gnaw on—like maybe your leg bone."

Arturo gave Baldassare a black look but said nothing.

Brother Danner said, "Arturo, do not worry about the black wolf. Brother Tristan is with us. He was standing behind me while you were facing down the beast. I am sure he would have done something if the wolf attacked you. I saw how he measured the distance between the wolf and his horse."

"Very funny, Brother Danner," I replied, smiling. "I noticed how you stood next to me and were looking for the nearest tree to climb as poor Arturo confronted the wolf."

Brother Danner laughed and replied, "I was trying to protect you. I saw how big your eyes were and how pale you looked. I thought your hair was starting to turn from red to white."

Ravenaire, in a teasing voice, said, "The wolf likes me." She had laughter in her sparkling eyes and a smug look on her face. "He is my friend. I do think he would protect me if I were in trouble, if our mighty warriors were not here."

Her words gave the men the feeling that as mighty as they were as warriors, there was always one who was the better. The wolf was unique. The beast was calmed by Ravenaire but could be a savage killer if the need arose. The wolf would protect her.

*

Just before evening, Scipio saw Night Hawk pick up the scent of men. The hairs on the wolf's back rose as he gave a low growl. Scipio was next to the beast and put a hand in the air to warn Hassan and the other Assassin, Aamil, of danger. Both Assassins dropped to their knees and crept slowly to the boy and his great beast. Fifty yards ahead, a French patrol of ten men on horseback were stopped by a stream to refresh their horses and fill their flasks with water.

Hassan crawled to within twenty-five yards of the men on the right, and Aamil crawled the same on the left. Scipio led Night Hawk to within forty yards, crawling on his belly. The beast slunk down and followed Scipio; his slanted yellow eyes never left the men he had scented. Slowly, Scipio released the leash of Night Hawk and gave a command to attack. Night Hawk silently charged the French soldiers.

One of the French soldiers, kneeling by the stream, looked up just as Night Hawk closed his fangs into the man's throat, knocking him to the ground. The French soldiers were surprised by the attack of the beast, but before they could come to the aid of the struggling soldier on the ground, arrows found their mark. Hassan quickly fitted another arrow to his bow, and another arrow buried deep into another French soldier. Aamil sent another arrow into a French soldier while Hassan drew his sword and charged the remaining soldiers. Aamil soon joined the fray. Scipio had his sword and dagger drawn and charged the French soldiers as well.

Night Hawk had killed three French soldiers and was attacking a fourth. With death closing in, three French soldiers pressed their horses to escape, but arrows found their mark. Aamil gathered up all the horses and tied their reins to a nearby tree so the horses did not alert the fortress from whence they had come. Hassan ruffled Scipio's hair and said to Aamil, "Scipio is becoming a good warrior, along with this beast."

Scipio responded, "Night Hawk is becoming a good Assassin," as he played with the wolf. The wolf reacted with fake growling and proceeded to knock all three men to the ground. The three Assassins smiled at one another in agreement. The men then picked themselves up and blended into the night, with the wolf in the lead.

CHAPTER 13

A DISCOVERY

A Serbian mercenary burst into Greco's villa. He was breathless and showed fear in his face as he rushed past servants and other mercenaries until he came to where Greco was.

Greco had just finished chopping off a man's finger and was gnawing on it, sucking the blood from the end. Greco said to the man, using the severed finger to point to him, "If you ever laugh at my face again, I will cut off your nose and your right ear with the gold earring." The man held his bloody hand and ran from Greco. Greco threw the well-chewed finger at the running man.

Greco walked over to another man, who was looking at the floor and did not want to meet Greco's eyes. Greco said to the man, "Too bad about Marinko losing his finger. I do not like his humor." Leaning into the Serbian mercenary, Greco made a quick move and sliced off the man's right ear. The man pulled away from Greco, holding the damaged side of his bloody head. Greco said, "I think it's funny that you are missing an ear and Marinko is missing a finger." The ear fell to the floor, and Greco stomped it with the heel of one of his heavy boots.

Greco then turned to the other terrified men. He laughed and encouraged the other men to laugh along with him. "No one laughs at Greco," he said, thumping his broad chest while looking at the other cutthroats.

The scene was not an isolated incident with his men. They were all terrified of him. Some had tried to run and escape Greco, but Greco always offered gold to those who found the escaped men. The captured men met slow deaths. The only things keeping them there were the gold and the promise of more gold. Some of the men had plotted to kill Greco, but somehow, Greco had found out. The plotters had been slowly killed in front of the others, piece by piece. The process had taken a few days. Greco had made sure the plotters did not bleed out right away. He had kept them barely alive until it no longer amused him. Then he had released the hounds to finish off the men.

Greco strode to a table that had some food on it, grumbling to himself, and sat down. He ate a hunk of cheese, dried fish, grapes, and some bread, with wine nearby, and then acknowledged his lookout man. "What is it, Darko?"

Darko replied excitedly, "My lord, friends spotted a small army of maybe one hundred fifty men about three miles away."

Greco replied calmly, "We have stayed clear of politics. No one bothers us. This is not my concern."

Darko replied, "My lord Greco, there are Templar knights, along with people in black scouting to the front and both flanks. We know who is close friends with the Templars and Assassins. The prince still lives and is hunting you down!"

Slamming a beefy fist on the table, causing the men in the room to jump, Greco replied, "I killed the Dark Prince with my crossbow. Maybe he is the devil, as the Assassins claim!"

Greco was visibly shaken by the news. He had fled to France because the French king, Philip IV, had put a price on the Dark Prince's head, and the Knights Templar had been disbanded from the church by order of the French pope, Clement V.

Greco stood up and shouted, "We have to leave immediately! Gather the rest of the men. We will go to the French fortress."

Greco thought, *They have five thousand men there. The Dark Prince, the heathen Assassins, and the dreaded Templar knights cannot reach us inside the fortress. We have enough gold to bribe the commander of the fortress. Besides, we have done a few favors for him. He owes us.*

"Once inside, if he does not see things the way I wish for him and his officers to see them, we will kill them as well. The French soldiers will answer to me, or each one of them will die a slow death till they do!" said Greco, shaking a fist in the air.

The fortress was located in a vast area of forests and glades and scattered farms and vineyards—a strategic location in the Aquitaine. If the area were taken by a foreign country, it would open a gateway to power into France. There were five thousand men-at-arms in the fortress. The area was being contested by the Basques at the time. England still desired to control the Aquitaine. The locals were unrestful but went about their business.

*

Jean-Luc saluted and said, "Lieutenant Bertrand, I am concerned about my missing patrol. They are overdue by two hours."

Lieutenant Bertrand had led men into combat against the Saracens in Arabia for more than ten years. A tall, lean man in his late thirties, he carried scars on his face and body as marks of valor. He led his men by example and was fearless in battle. A no-nonsense man, he demanded absolute fealty. Lieutenant Bertrand had been assigned to that post as a reward for his heroism and his value as an experienced officer.

The fortress in the Aquitaine was key to protecting France under Philip IV. All the men-at-arms were seasoned soldiers from different towns in the southwestern part of France, to reinforce its border in the west. Upon hearing Jean-Luc's news, Lieutenant Bertrand knew there was an enemy in his territory, a danger to the fortress and to the passageway into the heart of France.

Pacing back and forth, Lieutenant Bertrand pondered what to say to Captain Jules Laurent. Lieutenant Bertrand had wanted to increase the number of men in the patrols when he first heard of strange men in the vicinity. Captain Laurent had laughed at the idea, saying no one would dare attack the fortress. Lieutenant Bertrand did not enjoy that once again, he had been right in his assessment of a problem, and his superior, Captain Laurent, had been wrong.

The lieutenant and the captain had a history together. Nine years ago, the captain had given orders to kill all people in a small village outside Jerusalem. Lieutenant Bertrand had refused to follow his captain's orders. There had been a heated argument and a threat of severe consequences. The lieutenant had stood his ground and said he would not kill noncombatants. The captain had placed four soldiers to guard the lieutenant and then annihilated all in the village and left it in ashes.

Lieutenant Bertrand had been put in confinement for a month and then released and brought before Captain Laurent. The captain had had all his men present and addressed his lieutenant. Lieutenant Bertrand had been prepared for death, knowing Captain Laurent's temper and the way he made examples of soldiers who disobeyed him or failed to accomplish his objectives. However, surprisingly, Captain Laurent had given Lieutenant Bertrand a reprieve and had given him back his command. Nothing was said of it again. The lieutenant and the captain had established mutual respect and went on to work closely together.

Lieutenant Bertrand knocked at the door of Captain Laurent and said, "I need to speak with you on urgent business."

The door opened, and Lieutenant Bertrand entered the office. He noticed a large, ugly man sitting in a chair, drinking wine from a crystal glass.

The captain, blocking the lieutenant from entering farther into the room, said in an infuriated voice, "Please tell me what is so urgent."

The lieutenant stopped his salute and responded, "A patrol is long overdue. I feel something has happened."

"Send another patrol out to find the missing patrol! Why do I have to think for you? Get busy, and do your job!" shouted Captain Laurent.

The lieutenant saluted the captain, turned on his heel, and strode toward the door. He noticed the big, ugly man looked worried and had spilled some of his wine on his shirt. The lieutenant smiled as he left. The captain had overreacted with the news, and the ugly man looked frightened.

Jean-Luc, sergeant at arms, rushed to Lieutenant Bertrand as the lieutenant walked into the bailey. "Lieutenant Bertrand, two other patrols are missing. They have not reported back in over an hour!"

Lieutenant Bertrand was stunned. "Are you sure they are overdue? You are saying twenty men, plus the ten original men in the first patrol, are missing? How can that be? We are not at war with anyone. We would have heard of any large foreign army entering the Aquitaine. Let us check the map and see what sectors the three patrols were patrolling."

Under the cover of darkness, yellow eyes watched from a distance. During the blackest hour of the night, the wolf had found his prey. A soft, deep growl rumbled from the beast's throat as he picked up human scents. Blood stained the wolf's muzzle as he paced back and forth. Behind him were his bloodstained companions, also watching the fortress. Ten dead Frenchmen lay mutilated not far from the wolf. Soon there would be more dead Frenchmen.

In the early morning hours, Scipio, Night Hawk, and the two Assassins, Hassan and Aamil, made their way back to the Dark Prince's encampment. They had traveled twenty-three miles, traveling all night, until they staggered to the campfires and collapsed. Blood and gore covered their clothes. Their faces, arms, and hands were still oozing blood. I met the group as they entered the camp.

An Assassin went to Tamir's tent to tell him of the arrival of the patrol. Other Assassins went to the tent of the Dark Prince to tell him. Before long, the entire camp was alerted to the arrival of the men and beast, and all approached the center of the encampment to hear the news.

Water and food were brought to the exhausted men and beast. After the men drank and ate a little, they were ready to tell what they had seen and done. The beast wanted more chicken to eat. Those gathered feared for their lives. A couple of warriors rushed to the scullery and ordered more fowl for the beast to eat. Some of the warriors protested about food going to the beast and not to them. An Assassin strode over to the protesters and stood before them. The protests stopped.

The Dark Prince, Ravenaire, Brother Danner, Arturo, the mighty Baldassare, Dana DeFusco, Tamir, and I all sat in front by the fire and told the small patrol to tell their story. As Hassan, Aamil, and Scipio relayed the events and added to one another's stories, the black wolf added deep growls and barks, which brought grins from the warriors. Some said the wolf was actually trying to communicate.

The Dark Prince and I questioned the men about the patrols they had confronted and asked them to explain the outcome once again. Hassan retold the story of how they had taken the French by surprise. The black wolf had singled out one of the Frenchmen and attacked him. Hassan and Aamil had used their bows and arrows to pick off more Frenchmen. Scipio and the wolf had leaped into the fight and taken down more Frenchmen. Hassan and Aamil had finished off any who tried to escape with bow and arrow or knife. They had taken the French by surprise each time they attacked. A total of forty Frenchmen had been in the patrols. None of the Frenchmen had survived.

The Dark Prince and I conferred together for some minutes. The prince then turned to the others and said, "The French will send out more warriors to look for the men who killed their French patrols. The French will be swarming over the lands to punish us. We do not have enough men to confront the French. From what I have been told by our patrol, the fortress is large enough to hold five thousand men. We must kill their patrols, stop all supplies coming to the fortress, and pick off their men on the ramparts. It will be a siege that will last for an undetermined time. We will fight like the Assassins. We will be like ghosts. Like smoke. We will undermine their determination. We know Greco, a mosquito-bugger, is in the fortress. My spies tell me so. It will be a question as to how long the French will want to keep this up.

"I want the Templar knights to stay back until I need them, except for the monks Danner and Tristan. The Templar knights will stay back another mile. Do not be seen, and do not get into any trouble. I will call for you by sending a rider, an Assassin. He will find you. I want the rest of the men in teams of twenty. I want at least two Assassins in each team. Riders will coordinate between each team. We will be fluid among the teams. We will hit and run. Do not get into a prolonged fight with the French."

Danner looked over at me and said, "We sit at the sidelines. What say you?"

I replied, "I will miss the bashing."

The Dark Prince waved Dana DeFusco over to him. Dana strode over to the prince and said, "Yes, my liege?"

The Dark Prince studied Dana before answering. Dana stood close to the prince's height but was slender. He was built like a rapier, slim but deadly. There was a hidden strength in Dana. He was capable in attack and counterattack tactics. He was like a great cat waiting in ambush to take down prey bigger than itself.

The Dark Prince said softly, "I am saving your men till I need them. I know the Assassins are doing most of the work, but I have my reasons. Nothing is wrong. I know you are very capable in what you do. Ravenaire and I worry about you. If anything happened to you, it would devastate Ravenaire and me. Do not worry. Your time will come."

CHAPTER 14

GRECO

"Uncle Tristan, tell us the story about this evil man named Greco and our grandfather the Dark Prince. How did they meet?" asked Franco.

"Was that man as bad as Uncle Arturo and Uncle Baldassare say he was? I will make a wager that Uncle Baldassare could have defeated Greco," said Mark Anthony.

"I know Grandfather could have. No one beats the Dark Prince! I am sorry I did not include you, Uncle Tristan. I wager you could have beaten him too," said Rose Marie.

I recalled the stories surrounding Greco from many years ago.

*

A Greek fishing boat had beached on the sand of Cefalù, Sicily, after a stormy night. Some of the old wooden boards in the bottom of the boat were cracked and had sprung leaks. The two young men—Adonis, a good-looking and vain man, and Aridaios the Strong—were thankful they had made land in one piece. They had battled ten-foot waves and sixty-mile-an-hour winds for twelve hours. The two young men had lost all their catch and were exhausted from trying to steer the boat and bailing water all night during the storm.

The boat needed repairs. The rudder was broken, the mast was cracked, and the sails were torn. The boat was too heavy to drag above the high-tide mark because of all the water in it. The young men, with aching muscles, left the boat where it was, collapsed on the sand, and fell asleep.

When they woke, they were hungry and tired. It was midday, and the sun felt good. Their clothes were dry but sandy as they headed for the small fishing village to get something to eat and inquire about help with their boat.

In the village, Adonis and Aridaios were able to get a loaf of bread, a jug of new wine, a large hunk of cheese, and sardines. They were able to roast the sardines and finish off the bread and cheese by the waterfront. The wine was easy going down. The Greeks felt better after a good meal and wine. They had no more money but were willing to work for help on their boat. The taller Greek, Adonis, was incredibly strong. He sometimes used his size to intimidate others or beat them senseless for what he wanted, while Aridaios was a hard worker and honest man.

Several Sicilian sailors went to look at their boat and shook their heads. The tide had come in and was pounding the boat. It was slowly breaking up. The Sicilian men went back to their village, leaving the two Greeks standing on the beach, pondering what they were going to do.

After the villagers left, Adonis and Aridaios made their way down the coast to a large port, where they found work on a local fishing scow. The days passed quickly. They were making money and had a place to stay at a reasonable price.

Aridaios was saving money to return home, while Adonis wanted to stay. He was in love with a local girl, Calidonia Nicoluccia, and wanted to pursue her. She was indifferent to his advances. Her parents did not like foreigners and wanted her to marry a Sicilian.

One night, while Calidonia Nicoluccia was coming back from market, she was accosted and raped by an unknown assailant later proven to be Adonis. When she awoke from her ordeal, she felt wretched. Her parents were concerned that she had not returned home at the expected time, and they went looking for her. When they finally found her, Calidonia was disheveled and despondent. The parents brought her home and put her to bed after they cleaned her up. The mother rushed out to fetch the local wise-woman healer. When she arrived, the wise woman went straight to Calidonia's room and closed the door. An hour later, she came out and told the parents she had done all she could for Calidonia. Time would help heal her. Calidonia's father was furious about what had happened to his daughter and vowed to find the man and give him Sicilian justice.

Word spread throughout the entire village, and by midmorning, the men showed up at Signor Nicoluccia's house, ready to find the blasphemous man. They found that the big Greek Adonis was missing. A little while later, a boat was reported missing. Some of the fishermen wanted to sail after the Greek, but wiser heads held sway. The Greek had many hours' lead on them and would never be caught.

*

Greco grew up in an orphanage with strict discipline and no love. He was hated for the actions of his father, whom he never had known. His mother, Calidonia Nicoluccia, had died in childbirth. The baby, later to be called Greco for *Greek*, had survived. The name marked the baby for life as a reminder of what had happed to Calidonia, who had died in birth because of a Greek.

Greco did not know the meaning of love. He knew only strength and power and the desire to take what he could whenever he could. Greco had no friends and was considered an outsider.

Sixteen years later, the young man known as Greco watched a drunk man stagger from the Blue Snail tavern on his way home. The man was known to be carrying much coin from a heavy catch of fish earlier and had been celebrating his good fortune with his friends.

Adie, a small dark boy, whispered to Greco, "You can attack him when he rounds the corner. There is an alley where you can take his money. No one will see you."

Greco gave a crooked smile and smashed his big fists together. He punched Adie on the shoulder, making the smaller man stagger, and said, "You go to the other end of the alley, showing your blade. I will be at the other end and finish the job." Greco, standing six feet, three inches tall, with broad shoulders and the promise of a muscular body, waited patiently for the man to enter the alley.

At sixteen years old, Greco was scarred from the battles he had fought while growing up on the streets. He was an angry young man who never had known his father and was shunned by everyone in the town.

As leader of a young group of thugs, Greco ruled by muscle and brawn. In a few years, he gained more followers and soon controlled the waterfront. He had many scars, his nose had been broken countless times, and part of his right ear was missing. He had a thick purple scar running down the left side of his face, from his temple to his lower jaw, which throbbed when he was angry. Greco was a terrifying sight to meet up with at night or in an alley.

*

I sighed as the story of Greco unfolded in my mind.

"What say you, Uncle Tristan? Was he a scary man?" asked Rose Marie.

Franco said, "Greco must have known right from wrong."

Mark Anthony added, "I will wager he would knife you in the back."

Rose Marie quietly said, "I will wager he had no one to tuck him in bed and tell him nice stories."

I replied, "Yes, he was a scary man. But there is more to the story of your grandfather the Dark Prince."

*

The French controlled Sicily and ruled with an iron hand. The Sicilian people had to pay high taxes on almost all things bought or sold. French soldiers walked the streets of the cities with swagger and a strong contempt for the local people. The soldiers took many liberties with the women of Sicily, whether they were maidens or married. Sicilian men were killed while trying to defend the honor of their women.

During that troubled time, the Dark Prince, Arturo, and Baldassare were in Sicily, doing business with merchants interested in certain items from the Middle East. The three adventurers saw the injustices of the Sicilian people by the pompous French and did not like what they observed. The French also controlled Naples. The Dark Prince had been in trouble for dueling with French dignitaries and leaving a trail of dead French bodies in Naples. Death followed the Dark Prince as a faithful companion wherever he went.

The DeFusco family in Naples had many friends among the Sicilian nobility. The Dark Prince and his two cousins met with the nobility in a warehouse by the waterfront and organized a plan to oust the French in Sicily. The Dark Prince hoped he could do the same in Naples. The house of Rossi pledged four hundred men-at-arms, and the house of Ricci pledged 150 men-at-arms. Baron DeLuca and Baron Giordano each pledged two hundred men-at-arms. The Dark Prince pledged five hundred men-at-arms from Naples. All the nobles swore an oath of fidelity.

Palermo, Sicily, was a hotbed of furor for independence from France. When the fighting started, the Dark Prince, Arturo, and the mighty Baldassare were right in the middle of it. True to his word, the Dark Prince brought five hundred warriors from Naples and fought alongside Baron Rossi and his men. The fighting was vicious, and no quarter was given. The fight broke out in pockets all over the city. Barons Ricci, DeLuca, and Giordano were with their men, fighting in other areas of Sicily.

The Dark Prince, along with Arturo to his right and the mighty Baldassare to his left, found himself down by the waterfront. Prince Henry spotted a small pocket of French fighting one man. The prince nodded to the fight off to his left, and the three headed over to help the lone man.

The prince moved quickly to the side of the man, who was wounded in several places but continued to fight. The prince swung his sword, killing one soldier instantly. He then moved forward, taking on three French soldiers. The French soldiers smiled at one another as this man challenged all three of them. They attacked the prince in unison. The prince moved like a cat. The wounded man watched in amazement as the stranger defeated all three French soldiers in a matter of moments.

While the prince was talking to the wounded man, a fourth soldier came silently from behind and thrust his sword. Before the wounded man could warn the prince, the prince wheeled around to his left, dropped to one knee, and made a killing thrust into the man's chest. It all happened so fast the wounded man thought it was his imagination.

The wounded man asked the prince his name. The prince responded, "I am Henry DeFusco, the prince of Naples," making a sweeping, deep bow. The prince then straightened and asked, "And whom did I just rescue?"

The wounded man tried to stand a little taller. "I am called Greco. I control the waterfront. My men either died or fled when the French ran here from the city. I tried to stop the French, but my men just fled."

The man called Greco suddenly collapsed to the ground. Arturo and Baldassare killed the last of the French soldiers and came back to the prince. "Who is that man?" Arturo asked, pointing to the fallen Greco.

The prince responded, "He told me he is called Greco."

Baldassare said, "He is the ugliest man I have ever seen." Baldassare knelt down and felt for a heartbeat. "He is still alive; we should take him to a healer."

The prince saw a man creeping around a corner. The prince and Arturo strode over to the cautious man. The furtive man saw them coming toward him and was about to run, when he heard someone say, "If you run, you die."

The sneaky man stopped and slowly turned to face Arturo, who was standing within two feet of him and holding an Italian dagger in his hand, ready to throw or slash. The man put up his hands in surrender and stood still. The prince strode over to them and asked, "Are you one of Greco's men?"

The man nodded.

The prince reached into a fold of his clothes and pulled out a purse. He held some coins out, and the man's eyes glittered. "I give you these coins for Greco, who is lying on the ground over there." He pointed to Baldassare and the fallen Greco. "I want you to get Greco to a healer. Make sure you do this and he lives. I know people, and you will not live very long if Greco dies. Now, go get Greco help."

Shortly, a group of people suddenly appeared. They hurried over to Greco and picked him up. The prince made eye contact with Greco's man and pointed two fingers to his own eyes and then to the other man's eyes. The man nodded and got everyone moving quickly.

*

"Why would Grandfather help Greco? He always kills people he fights," said Mark Anthony.

"Maybe Grandfather had a stomachache and did not feel like it," said Franco.

Rose Marie said, "I know why! Our grandfather did not want to get his sword dirty!"

CHAPTER 15

GRECO AND THE DARK PRINCE

At the hour of vespers on Easter, March 30, 1282, the War of the Sicilian Vespers ensued. The people of Palermo, with the help of the barons, slaughtered two thousand French. As rioting broke out, news spread quickly around the island, and revolt became evermore widespread. Within one year, Sicily became free of French rule.

I reflected on a visit from Greco to the Dark Prince. It was the second time they had met. The first time they had met, the Dark Prince had saved Greco's life, fighting the French for freedom.

Two years later, after the Sicilian Vespers, Greco and a companion named Calamaretto sailed from Palermo to Naples to visit the Dark Prince. Calamaretto was a short, wiry man with many scars on his arms from street fights. His face had a scar across his left cheek to his ear. He was a shifty man who would stab anyone in the back if he thought the person had any money. Calamaretto never came face-to-face with an opponent but worked from the shadows and from behind. He had killed many men and some women. He went along with Greco because he thought the trip might be profitable. He was also afraid of Greco. When Greco asked someone to do something, the alternative was a painful death.

The trip was uneventful, with calm seas and a following wind to fill the sails. In Naples, the two men rented two horses and rode to the gates of the fortress. Greco spoke to Calamaretto softly. "Do not say anything. I will do all the talking. Keep your eyes and ears open. Do not cut anyone with that knife of yours."

Calamaretto returned a sly smile and would not look Greco in the eye.

The prince greeted Greco and Calamaretto and welcomed them to the fortress. Regent Mattiano, Prince Henry's father, felt an immediate distrust of Greco and even more so of Calamaretto. Regent Mattiano looked questioningly at Prince Henry as to his friendship with the two ruffians. The regent often questioned the friends the prince associated with. Lady Serafina nervously clutched her pearl necklace while absently making the hand sign of the devil behind her back. She felt anxious, with a brooding fear boiling up in her.

During the course of the day, Prince Henry guided Greco and Calamaretto through the fortress. Arturo and the mighty Baldassare followed from a distance. Both of the cousins had a bad feeling about Prince Henry's guests.

Several days later, Lady Serafina discovered some of her jewelry was missing. She told her husband, Regent Mattiano, who became furious. Being a DeFusco, Regent Mattiano had a quick temper that, when pushed, was deadly to the provoker. Regent Mattiano immediately ordered a search of the fortress and all people who were not of the family or nobility.

After a thorough search of the fortress, Regent Mattiano ordered all who were not family to go to the great hall. Soldiers were dispatched to all entryways of the fortress to ensure no one left until the jewelry was found.

Prince Henry DeFusco, Greco, Greco's companion, Arturo, and the mighty Baldassare were in the stables. Greco walked his horse from its stall, while his companion looked at the horses in the stalls nearby, thinking about stealing one and making a profit from the sale.

A guard came out of the fortress, looking for the prince. The prince was not in the great hall, where all the others had gathered. The guard hailed the prince and spoke of a theft of jewels from Lady Serafina. The prince turned to Greco and saw a flicker of guilt. The prince started to approach Greco, when he saw Calamaretto mount a horse and gallop toward the main road.

The prince called out to the mighty Baldassare to stop Calamaretto. Baldassare ran toward the charging warhorse and was able to grab the horse's neck as it sprinted past him. Baldassare was jerked off his feet as he tackled the two-thousand-pound horse. The horse fell hard onto its side, throwing its rider to the ground. Greco moved toward the prince, hefting the hatchet he always carried on his belt.

Greco said in a deadly voice, "Get out of my way, little prince. I will leave bloody chunks of you all over the ground for the dogs to eat if you do not."

The prince drew his dagger and said, "This is how you repay me? I saved your life, and now you steal from my family. Prepare to visit hell."

The two men circled each other each, looking for an opening. Arturo helped Baldassare up from the horse he had just tackled, watching Calamaretto closely. Calamaretto frantically looked for any way to escape but was kept at bay by Arturo and the sword pointed at his chest.

The sounds of combat turned everyone's head. Greco made a lunge at the prince, and his hatchet made a sweeping arc through the air, just missing the prince. The prince, in a catlike move, countered with a vicious slash with his dagger, cutting the side of Greco down to his ribs. Greco cried out in pain, holding his side with his free hand. Blood seeped through his fingers and dripped onto the ground.

Greco's face contorted into a savage smile as he tried to close in on the prince, saying, "I am going to kill you now!"

The will-o'-the-wisp Prince dodged another sweeping slash. Greco swung again and again with vicious swipes of the deadly hatchet blade but could not touch the demon-quick moves of the prince. A quick slash to Greco's leg at midthigh and another to his left cheek left the bleeding and frustrated man quickly realizing his mortality. The prince threw a hard punch to Greco's jaw with his free hand, dropping him to the ground. The prince moved quickly behind Greco and put his dagger to Greco's throat, making a light cut with the sharp-edged dagger and drawing a thin line of blood as he moved the dagger across Greco's throat.

The prince said to Greco, "Make any move, and I will kill you. This fight is over." He kicked Greco in his backside, knocking him flat on his face. The prince put a boot on Greco's back to humiliate Greco, holding him on the ground.

Everyone in the great hall had come out to watch the fight after the guard rushed inside to tell of the prince and Greco. Regent Mattiano and his brothers, their wives, servants, nobles, and soldiers all looked on as the prince put Greco to the ground. I glanced at Danner with a knowing look. Danner just shook his head. We all marveled at how fast the prince moved. There was never any doubt the prince would not lose to Greco.

Prince Henry DeFusco had won many tournaments throughout Europe and was considered the greatest swordsman of them all. All the family and nobles who had watched the confrontation with the prince, who used only his dagger, said with great pride what a foolish man Greco was to take on the prince.

Those gathered spoke in awe of Baldassare for the way he had tackled a running warhorse, confirming how strong he was. There had been no hesitation in his tackling a running two-thousand-pound warhorse. The family pointed out how quickly Arturo had held the companion of Greco at sword point so he could not escape. Lady Serafina said, "It was magnificent to see my son, the prince, and his two cousins, Arturo and the mighty Baldassare, fight together to protect each other."

Arturo and the mighty Baldassare walked over to the prince, prodding Greco's companion at sword point. The prince told Greco, "Stand up. We are going to the great hall to see what you have stolen."

Greco responded, "A few jewels will not be missed by your family."

The prince gave a hard shove that made Greco stumble.

When everyone had assembled back in the great hall and order was restored, Regent Mattiano said to Greco, "You are banished from my lands. If you come back, my men have orders to kill you."

Greco looked sullen and beaten. His side was still bleeding, and he had a thin red line around his neck like a necklace. The jewels were found and returned to Lady Serafina. Soldiers moved forward to escort the bloody Greco to the docks and see him on his way.

Greco's companion bent down as if he had an insect bite on his lower leg. He came up with a boot knife in his hand and was about to throw it at Regent Mattiano's back, when he staggered back, holding his throat and dropping his dagger. The prince's dagger had found its mark. Everyone turned to watch as Calamaretto fell to the floor, jerking in his death throes as blood gushed from his throat. The prince strode over to the companion, pulled the dagger from the body, wiped the blade on the dead man's clothes, and said to Greco, "Next time I see you, you are a dead man."

Soldiers roughly grabbed the bloody Greco and escorted him out of the fortress. They marched Greco to the docks of Naples and ensured he was put on a boat sailing to Sicily.

Everyone started talking at once to the prince. Regent Mattiano, Arturo, Baldassare, and others asked the prince at once, "Why did you not kill Greco?"

The prince smiled and replied, "I felt sorry for Greco. He has had a hard life. His mother died at childbirth, his father ran off, and he has no family. He grew up on the back streets of Sicily, learning to survive. I thought I could make a difference with the man. Alas, I see now I could not."

Arturo turned to the mighty Baldassare and said, "You did well in stopping Calamaretto. I was surprised you missed Calamaretto and tackled the horse. Maybe your eyesight is not so good. What say you?"

Baldassare replied, "You were in the way, as usual. But maybe we could try this again. You get on your horse and ride past, and I will tackle you as you ride by. I know you have a hard time getting on your horse. I will get a big box for you to stand on."

They both laughed. Arturo did not want to be tackled by Baldassare. There would have been many broken bones. Arturo said softly to Baldassare, "You know that in all the fights the prince has fought, Greco is the only person to live after fighting the prince."

Baldassare responded, "I do not think this is over between Greco and the prince. I think there will be another time when the prince is confronted by Greco, and the prince will not be so generous."

*

Mark Anthony exclaimed, "Uncle Baldassare tackled a horse!"

Franco said, "Our grandfather the Dark Prince beat that vile Greco with a dagger! He did not need a sword!"

Rose Marie added, "Our grandfather saved the day by throwing a knife and killing Calamaretto—and then wiping his knife on the dirty clothes of him. He saved his father's life!"

I smiled and said, "Yes, the Dark Prince and Baldassare did all that. But do not forget that Uncle Arturo was there and helped."

CHAPTER 16

GRECO AND THE POOR SOLDIERS GUILD

A year after the fiasco in Naples with the DeFusco family, in which Prince Henry DeFusco almost had killed him for trying to take some jewels, Greco was still planning vengeance. His fight with the prince of Naples had been one-sided. The prince was too quick with the dagger and had toyed with Greco. Greco had forgotten the speed of the prince, which he had demonstrated when he fought off four French soldiers to save Greco.

Greco had been humiliated in front of the entire royal court and the peasants who worked there. It had taken many weeks for the wounds he had received to stop bleeding and heal. Greco had not known if he was going to live or not. *Well*, Greco thought, *I have several scars from the prince to add to my collection. Scars that will remind me and fester with me forever.*

The following year, a German army was on the march to Naples. The prince of Naples had pushed too far by killing the fifteenth French ambassador in a duel. France was in control of the city-state of Naples. Killing a French ambassador was like attacking the king of France. The French king, Philip the Fair, put a price of one thousand gold pieces on the head of Prince Henry. Greco felt he could get back at the DeFusco family by helping the German army get through the defenses of the fortress of Naples. The trusting prince previously had shown Greco around the fortress.

During the year, Greco had to fight a challenger to his leadership of the Poor Soldiers Guild. The fight took place down at the docks, in an abandoned warehouse the Poor Soldiers Guild used for nefarious reasons. Greco's opponent, Stanek, was a seasoned warrior, a mercenary who killed for pay. Stanek had killed hundreds in Eastern Europe, fighting over their city-states. He liked to watch the light go out of the eyes of those he killed. Stanek had killed one too many people and had to flee from Eastern Europe to Sicily a few years back.

Standing six foot two and weighing 250 pounds of knotted muscle, Stanek was a formidable fighter. He preferred a sword from his country called a falchion, a one-handed, single-edged sword of European origin whose design was reminiscent of the Persian scimitar. The weapon combined the weight and power of an ax with the versatility of a sword. It had been developed from farmers' and butchers' knives of the sea type or in the manner of the larger messer, which had a heavy single blade. The shape concentrated more weight near the end, thus making it more effective for chopping strikes like an ax or cleaver.

Five hundred men crowded into the warehouse, yelling for the fight to start. They enjoyed the blood sport of the Poor Soldiers Guild. Greco was accompanied by an Arab assassin named Ya Mumeed the Slayer. Greco whispered to the Arab, "Did you bring the blowgun, as I asked you to?"

The assassin replied, "Allah has brought to you an instrument of surprise to help you in this fight. Allah will be the guiding light for me to see clearly and vanquish your enemy."

Greco replied, "Stay close, but let no one see you."

Ya Mumeed replied, "Your wish shall be granted. No one will see. The poison dart will work swiftly." The assassin bowed slightly to Greco and melted into the noisy crowd.

Three days later, Greco ordered a meeting of the Poor Soldiers Guild. He wanted to reinforce his leadership with the men. The men were still talking about the fight quietly among themselves. Something seemed a little odd in the way Stanek had fallen to Greco's hatchet. The men of the Poor Soldiers Guild, numbering close to five thousand, were surprised Greco had defeated Stanek. Most of them secretly had wanted Greco to lose, but none had the courage to challenge him.

A week after Greco's meeting with the Poor Soldiers Guild, Prince Henry, Arturo, Danner, the mighty Baldassare, and I arrived by boat late at night and found the warehouse where their meeting was being held. The prince and his men who were following entered with a flourish as the big warehouse doors slammed open. The prince strode forward with a smile and confidence, approaching Greco, who was standing on a makeshift platform. The prince brushed aside or shoved men who got in his way or tried to impede him, to stand in front of Greco. Arturo and Baldassare followed behind the prince, as did Danner and I.

Greco shouted in a shaky voice, "What do you want, my dear old friend Henry DeFusco, prince of Naples?"

One could have heard a pin drop amid the silence. The men were amazed that the stranger had boldly walked into their meeting unafraid and was royalty.

The prince gave a deep bow. "My dear *amico*, I come in peace." The prince put his hands on his hips and said, "I have a proposition for you. A German army is heading for Naples, and I am looking for men to help fight them."

Greco laughed and looked at his men, bringing his arms up for his men to laugh with him. After the laughing subsided, Greco turned to the prince and said, "How much gold are you offering to us to fight?"

The prince became angry and replied, "I and the five hundred knights I brought with me to fight the French and save your life did not ask for gold."

Greco shrugged and said, "My men do not fight for nothing. Show me some gold, and maybe we will talk."

The men of the Poor Soldiers Guild had mixed reactions. Some were grateful the French no longer ran their lives. Others felt they had no responsibility to go to Naples and fight a German army for someone else.

The prince stepped forward and said, "Maybe it would be better if I challenged you to the leadership of this guild right now."

Greco backed up on the makeshift platform. He did not want to fight the prince again. He realized not all his men agreed with him, and some wanted to see him fight the prince. He noticed the prince moving toward him and hastily said, "My prince, are you and your little group of men hoping to leave here alive? There are only five of you. We are one thousand here tonight."

The prince grimly replied, "You will be the first to die then. Another twenty-five or thirty will die soon after."

Thus, the prince was pledged 550 men to return to Naples with him and another eight hundred to follow.

*

Franco said, "Our grandfather had a lot of courage to walk into a thief's den unafraid and challenge the despot Greco!"

Mark Anthony said, "Greco was afraid of our grandfather the Dark Prince."

Rose Marie asked, "Uncle Tristan, were you afraid?"

The twin brothers immediately asked, "Uncle Tristan, were you afraid?"

I stood up from the chair and said, "I, Tristan du Lyonesse, a Knight Templar and adviser to the Dark Prince, would have fought to the death to save him. You see"—I bent down to the children—"bashing is what I do best."

The children all laughed and said, "Oh, Uncle Tristan."

CHAPTER 17

GRECO'S REVENGE

A few months later, Greco arrived in the port of Naples. There was chaos everywhere as a German army put the fortress of Naples under siege. The port was safe because the fortress guarded the port, and the navy of Naples controlled the Bay of Naples. The fortress walls were forty-five feet high and four feet thick. There were several tall, round turrets on all four sides of the fortress for the archers, along with murder holes for archers and crossbowmen to shoot from. The gatehouse had a heavy wooden door at the inner opening, which soldiers had shut and locked with braces. The barbican was built of stone and had towers with arrow loops and battlements from which archers shot arrows. The Italians were fighting a defensive battle, led by an army from Frederick I Barbarossa, king of Germany and holy Roman emperor. General Otto von Wolfgang was known as the Iron Heel and had never been defeated.

Because of the hundreds of excellent archers on the walls and at the turrets and murder holes, the Germans could not live long as they approached the walls of the fortress. Hundreds of bodies lay at the foot of the walls, with multiple arrows protruding from them. The Iron Heel called a retreat for the third time, frustrated that his army could not penetrate the fortress's defenses.

Greco was able to follow the retreating army and mix with them till they returned to their encampment half a mile away, a little farther than the range of a longbow. Meandering around the German encampment, Greco looked for the officers' quarters. As he did not speak German, it took Greco a while to find the officers.

The strange man was visibly upset as two soldiers came up to him, seized him by sword point, and led him to the officers. The officers were curious and started to question him in German. Greco tried to explain in Sicilian why he was there. No one understood, and the Germans became more suspicious.

General Otto von Wolfgang, the Iron Heel, strode up to the ugly man and stopped within a foot of him. The general watched him closely like a hawk watching its prey and said in German, "Beggar, what do you want here? Why are you trying to spy on us? I can have you executed right now if you do not answer me!"

A terrified Greco stammered in Sicilian, "I came to help you enter the fortress. I know secret ways into it."

A young officer who had spent time in Italy said to the general, "This beggar says he can lead us into the fortress."

The other officers laughed at the notion that the ugly man could do what he said. One of the officers asked, "Will he fly us into the fortress?" With that, the officers laughed till tears came to their eyes. Even the ramrod general laughed.

Greco was confused and did not understand why the Germans were laughing. He tried to stay calm but was starting to feel angry. *What are these crazy Germans thinking? I do not like to be laughed at. I am offering my services and knowledge, and they laugh at me! These Germans keep calling me something I do not understand, and I think it is an insult. I will wait my time.*

General Otto von Wolfgang told his officers, "Take the beggar to where some of the Serbians are chained, and chain him as well to one of the poles. I will deal with him later. If he is telling the truth, we shall see, but if he is lying, then you men will practice your sword thrusts on him."

*

The general was upset. It was a week later, and the Germans had not made any progress in taking the fortress. The Germans brought in siege machines to break down the walls of the fortress, but in a daring raid, the Italian foot soldiers flanking the heavy cavalry burst through the surprised German force and torched the machines, leaving them useless. The Italians had to fight their way back to the fortress, losing many foot soldiers along the way, until they came within range of the longbow men, who gave them cover till the foot soldiers were safely inside the fortress. The heavy cavalry all made it back unscathed.

The Iron Heel was outraged. He hammered his fists together and roared to his officers, "I want this fortress to be in rubble in the next three days—or else!"

Inside his tent, the general summoned his four greatest knights: Sir Baldemarus, the brave one; Sir Rudolfus, the glory of the wolf; Sir Hartmannus, the bold one; and Sir Wilhelmus, the faithful protector. The general stood up from his table and approached the knights.

"Tomorrow I want you four knights to organize the army into four parts. The army will attack all four walls. They will bring ladders to climb the walls and get inside the fortress. We have an army of ten thousand. We will overwhelm the fortress, and victory will be ours. I do not want you four to climb the walls, just the soldiers. Our infamous Teutonic knights we have in reserve will break down the gatehouse and barbican at the same time. The Italians will be so busy defending the walls and gates they will not be looking anywhere else. This ugly beggar who wandered into our camp has shown me where the secret passages are located. I want the four of you and some trusted men to enter and bring me hostages of nobility."

The next day, the German army charged the fortress in full strength. As the army advanced, when they came within two hundred yards, arrows from the archers at their posts in the fortress took a toll. Hundreds of German foot soldiers met their early deaths. The German cavalry waited on the sidelines for their foot soldiers to start scaling the walls. Certain death awaited German soldiers advancing near the fortress walls.

Eventually, by sheer mass of troops, the German foot soldiers put up the ladders and started to climb. The general was happy to see his soldiers reach the walls of the fortress. He ordered his cavalry to attack, and they advanced. The Teutonic knights were in position and ready to attack. The clarion of a trumpet was heard by all on the battlefield and made the German host pause in wonder. Templar knights suddenly appeared from both sides of the fortress and charged into the German footmen from the right and left. The Templars swept the field with precision in a cavalry charge of lances and warhorses. The German general was surprised and outraged. He shook his fist at the Templar knights, promising to punish any Templars caught and held prisoner.

The Iron Heel was surprised that Templar knights were in Naples. *How did they get here? Why are they fighting for Naples? What rewards have been promised to them? Who is responsible for the Templars' being here? This changes everything. Why did not the French king tell me of this? General Otto von Wolfgang was fighting for France to stamp out this Italian city-state under French control for gold.*

The Iron Heel was at Acre with his army, but orders from the German king, Frederick Barbarossa, told him to pull out. In the middle of the night, per the message he had received from Frederick Barbarossa, the Iron Heel left in disgrace, following orders. The Templar knights refused to leave the battle.

The Templar knights were the most fearsome warriors in all of Europe and the Middle East. The Knights Templar, or the Poor Knights of Christ and of the Temple of Solomon, were a religious military order of knighthood established at the time of the Crusades. They had become a model and inspiration for other military orders.

Originally founded to protect Christian pilgrims to the Holy Land, the order had assumed greater military duties during the twelfth century. Its prominence and growing wealth, however, had provoked opposition from rival orders. Following the success of the First Crusade in 1095–99, a number of Crusader states had been established in the Holy Land, but those kingdoms had lacked the necessary military force to maintain more than a tenuous hold over their territories.

Most Crusaders had returned home after fulfilling their vows, and Christian pilgrims to Jerusalem had suffered attacks from Muslim raiders. Pitying the plight of the Christians, eight or nine French knights, led by Hugh de Payns, had vowed in late 1119 or early 1120 to devote themselves to the pilgrims' protection and to form a religious community for that purpose.

Baldwin II, king of Jerusalem, had given them quarters in a wing of the royal palace in the area of the former Temple of Solomon, from which they had derived their name. In 1139, Pope Innocent II had issued a bull that granted the order special privileges: the Templars were allowed to build their own oratories and were not required to pay the tithe or taxes; they were also exempt from episcopal jurisdiction, being subject to the pope alone, not to any kings or nobility of any country. The Knights Templar reported only to the pope.

During the Crusades, the fortress in the desert at Acre, the last Christian stronghold, had held only eight hundred knights, most of whom were Templars. The Teutonic knights had left suddenly one night, fearing the vast Muslim army approaching. The eight hundred Templar knights had fought off the 350,000-strong Muslim army for three months. Saladin, the leader of the Muslim army, in frustration, had come to terms with the grand master of the Templar knights, and the survivors had been allowed safe passage to the seaport to sail to Cyprus.

General Otto von Wolfgang observed that Sir Rudolfus, the glorious wolf, broke ranks and charged the remaining Templar knight leaving the field of battle. The Templar turned to meet the challenge and drew his sword. The sword hilt gave off a purple flash as sunlight hit the amethysts in the hilt. The Templar knight was Brother Danner, sword master of the brotherhood. He was a seasoned knight who had fought in the Middle

East and had been one of the last Templar knights to leave Acre. The last fortress in the desert held Christians who sought protection from the vast Muslim army of Saladin.

Sir Rudolfus and the Templar knight Danner clashed on the battlefield. They battled on horseback from late morning to early afternoon. Back and forth, the two opposing knights clashed. The men from one side would cheer, and then, a moment later, the opposing side would cheer. It looked as if the Templar knight had the advantage with his skill with the sword. Oh, how the sword sparkled purple with the amethysts in the hilt.

Templar knight Danner, riding a magnificent black stallion of the desert breed, was more agile and caused Sir Rudolfus numerous wounds. The German knight, weak and wounded, was mortally struck down by a final thrust of Danner's flashing sword.

Sir Hartmannus rode forth and challenged the weary Brother Danner, who was riding his powerful black stallion back to the fortress. The German side cheered as the challenge was given. Templar knight Danner turned and rode his steed to the German knight, and rules were spoken and accepted. There was honor among knights and most of the nobility. Danner raised his sword to the fortress, signifying his acceptance, and the fortress cheered.

The two knights separated and rode one hundred yards apart. Both knights raised their free hand and then charged each other. The ring of steel on steel, the screaming of the warhorses, the churning up of great clods of sod, and the fury of the combatants added to the drama of the life-and-death struggle of two valiant warriors.

Suddenly, in one of the wild charges between the two combatants, Danner was unhorsed. The German side gave great cheers as Danner lay on the ground. Sir Hartmannus rode his horse slowly down the German line and received cheers and shouted accolades from all. The Templar knight slowly moved. He was stunned from a blow to the head and was dizzy. His black stallion walked over to him and licked his face as the knight lay on the ground. Slowly, Danner came to his senses and stood.

Sir Hartmannus became aware of the standing Templar knight and turned his warhorse and charged. Danner was struck again by the heavy sword arm of Sir Hartmannus and went down again. Sir Hartmannus raised both arms up in victory and again rode slowly down the German line, accepting the cheers once again. Across the way, the Germans saw a black knight, Prince Henry DeFusco, struggling to get past his men to step out onto the field of honor to fight Sir Hartmannus. Danner once again made it to his unsteady feet and held on to his horse for support. Sir Hartmannus turned and could not believe the Templar knight was standing. He urged his charger on to kill this bothersome Templar once and for all. Danner moved away from his horse, drew his dagger, and waited. Danner's timing was perfect as he leaped up and pulled Sir Hartmannus to the ground.

The Templar was on top of Sir Hartmannus and asked the German knight to yield. Sir Hartmannus, with the dagger to his throat, refused to yield. Danner asked him one more time to yield. Sir Hartmannus struggled but could not break free. Sir Hartmannus was furious that he was on the ground with the Templar holding a dagger to his throat. He defiantly told the Templar he would not yield. The Templar said to him, "May God have mercy on your soul," and cut his throat. Sir Hartmannus was defiant to the end.

Danner slowly stood up and stumbled to his horse. He held on to the horse, and both slowly walked toward the fortress. There was silence on the field of honor. No German tried to stop or challenge the Templar knight as he slowly made his way back to the fortress. When the Templar made it to the far side of the field, Prince Henry DeFusco caught the Templar in his arms and carried him off the remaining field.

*

Greco guided the German soldiers through the fortress via the secret passageways he had learned about from the innocent Prince Henry. The group of Germans made their way silently and stealthily. He guided the Germans to Mattiano's room, and they battered the door in.

Regent Mattiano put up a fight using sword and dagger and killed the first two attackers. Mattiano's trusted hound took down a third German soldier. Lady Serafina had been told to hide in a closet before the door was broken down, and she stayed quiet. A German soldier hit Mattiano on the head with the hilt of his sword and watched Mattiano crumple to the floor. He then stabbed the hound in the chest as the hound sprang at him.

The German soldiers captured Mattiano as a prisoner, along with his five brothers, and escaped back through the secret passageways. The brothers had been taken by surprise and tried to fight from their own rooms in the fortress, but to no avail. Sir Angelo had a nasty head wound after being hit by the hilt of a sword while trying to fight off four German soldiers. The mighty Amadeo was taken down by the German soldiers and subdued by a heavy hit to the back of his head. Sir Mark Anthony was taken from behind but managed to fight until a sword struck his shoulder, causing him to drop his sword. Sir Genaro heard some noise outside his room and came out to investigate. He was met with a hard blow to his forehead by the hilt of a German sword and collapsed. Sir Joseph was taken in much the same way as Sir Genaro, by a hard blow to the forehead from the sword hilt of a German soldier. Sir Salvatore was attacked by German soldiers and subdued by many punches. He was finally hit on the top of his head with the pommel of a sword.

German General Otto von Wolfgang wanted the DeFusco males taken alive for ransom. The general realized he could not take the fortress, but he could pay for his troops and pocket some money for himself in a ransom. *The impetuous son of Regent Mattiano, Prince Henry, will come to terms with me, or he shall see his family executed. He brought this all upon himself with the duels he fought, including killing fifteen different ambassadors of the French king, Philip the Fair, over the last two years. Prince Henry stirred up the nobles' sons of Naples and beyond with the foolish notion that Naples should be run by Italians, not the king of France. The prince is a true wolf's head.*

Greco made friends with the Serbian assassins brought to Naples by General Otto von Wolfgang as part of his army. The Serbs and the Germans did not get along and were always at one another's throats. Some of the more militant Serbs were chained to posts for all the others to see as an example to all who disagreed with the general. When Greco was chained to a post, the Serbs immediately accepted him.

*

The general was not doing well in trying to defeat the men in the fortress. His siege machines had been destroyed, and the fortress had many archers to hold off any attacks. In addition, the fortress held Templar knights. The Templar knight with the flashing purple-hilted sword, riding that beautiful black stallion, had destroyed the confidence of the German knights. He had defeated two of the best knights the general had, an unheard-of victory. How could his army fight Templar knights if that one Templar knight could defeat so easily two of his best knights?

Ransom! The general knew he could not win, but a ransom of the DeFusco family would save face for him and pay for his army. Greco, accompanied by the German soldiers, arrived late in the day with their captive DeFusco brothers. The general was delighted. He had a big smile as he approached the prisoners.

General Otto von Wolfgang strode up to Regent Mattiano DeFusco until their faces were within inches of each other and said, "I will break you and reduce your fortress to rubble. My men will have sport with your women, and I will personally drag your cowardly son through the town of Naples after I hang him in the public square."

Regent Mattiano laughed and then spit in the face of the general. "My son, the Dark Prince of Naples, will kill you and drive your army out of Naples. You are already beaten but do not know it."

The general was livid. He motioned for two of the guards to chain Regent Mattiano to the whipping post. After the regent was secured to the post, the general snarled at him and said, "Let us see how you like the flogging!"

A burly German soldier came forward with a whip and waited for orders.

The general smiled and said to the regent, "Let's see how long your Italian hide lasts with the whip. Strip off his shirt so we may enjoy the bloody marks of the whip strokes. I want to hear this man scream and cry for mercy."

The DeFusco brothers all yelled and fought their bindings to try to stop the flogging. They were met with clubs beating them into submission. Bloodied and battered, the brothers could only look on with horror as Mattiano was whipped unmercifully.

Greco laughed. It felt good to watch the other man suffer. He spat at Regent Mattiano as he walked past him and strode up to General Otto von Wolfgang.

The general looked at Greco in distaste and said sardonically, "Well, what do you want, beggar?"

Greco smiled, held out a hand, and said, "Give me the gold you promised me for delivering the DeFusco brothers to you. Your battle is won."

The general answered trenchantly, "You get nothing, you filthy beggar. Get out of my sight, and leave this camp immediately, or you will get the same as him." He nodded to the regent.

Greco could not believe his ears. He grabbed the general's arm and said, "You promised me gold if I could deliver the brothers. I have done that. Where is my gold?"

The general pulled his arm out of the grasp of Greco and replied, "Get out of here now. If I see you again, I will have you drawn and quartered and fed to the dogs!"

Greco slunk out of sight from the general's eyes and went to his newfound Serbian friends. He gathered them around himself and spoke of gold.

*

The next morning, a lone rider carrying a white flag on a staff rode up to the fortress. The prince of Naples, Henry DeFusco, watched the rider approach and passed the word to allow the rider to advance unharmed. The rider rode to the base of the fortress and stopped. He called out to speak with the prince of Naples on behalf of General Otto von Wolfgang.

Prince Henry DeFusco stepped into view and said, "Tell the general I want my family members returned immediately! The general is a coward! He hides behind an army of buffoons. I will fight him man-to-man on the field of honor and leave his bones to the wolves to gnaw on. Tell him to go home, as he tires us with his army, scrounging for food and eating his own horses while he camps at my doorstep. Return my relatives unharmed."

The messenger replied, "General Otto von Wolfgang demands gold in return for your family members. Two wagons full. If not, your relatives will be executed this evening. The general will receive the gold if you value the lives of your relatives. There will be more executions in the future if General Otto von Wolfgang does not receive two wagonloads of gold."

The prince spoke softly to Dana DeFusco on his right side. "Dana, did we secure the secret passageways and put additional soldiers at each entrance with bowmen?"

Dana replied, "Yes, my prince. It has been done."

Prince Henry turned to a bowman nearby and said, "Bowman, can you put an arrow in the staff with the white flag the messenger has?"

The bowman studied the distance of the messenger and the small width of the staff the man carried and replied, "Yes, my lord. I can send an arrow into the staff. Do you want me to send another arrow someplace else, my lord?"

"No, bowman. Shoot only one arrow," replied the prince.

The messenger yelled out sarcastically, "I am waiting for a reply! I did not mean to frighten all within the fortress and leave everyone speechless."

The arrow hit the staff with force, piercing it and the messenger's hand. In pain, the messenger would have dropped the staff but could not.

Prince Henry bellowed, "You have my answer. The next arrow will pierce your miserable hide. I will meet your general on the field of honor within the hour to discuss the release on my terms. Now, leave my sight, and tell your master we are not to be blackmailed or intimidated by his puppet army."

The rider turned his horse and rode back to the German lines as if the devil were chasing him. He was terrified.

The prince of Naples called out, "Sir Danner, Tristan, Arturo, Baldassare, get ready to join me on the field of honor within the hour!"

An hour later, the prince and his companions rode out slowly in a straight line on desert-bred horses. The prince, Sir Arturo, and the mighty Sir Baldassare were dressed in chain mail, with the colors of their family coats of arms attached to their helmets and carrying battle swords and shields. The shields had their coats of arms painted on them. Sir Danner and I wore our Templar robes, and our shields were black, with the red Templar cross on them.

The Germans wore plate armor and rode on big warhorses. Their shields had their coats of arms painted on them, and they wore the colors of their houses on their helmets. The two groups stopped ten feet apart in the middle of the field. No one said anything as we studied one another, sizing up our opponents. The Germans smiled as they looked upon the Italians riding on smaller horses and wearing only chain mail. The Germans felt superior and contemptuous of their counterparts, except for the two Templar knights.

The general spoke in a contemptuous voice. "Which one of you is the prince of this decrepit land?"

Prince Henry replied, "I am the prince of Naples. Release my relatives immediately, or we will ruin your army and embarrass your puppet king! I want you and your cabbage-head army to leave immediately. The foul smell of you and your swine is upsetting our women and children. I know you and your men are accustomed to eating fish heads, animal excrement, and entrails. We can smell you from several leagues away."

The general was beside himself. His face became beet red, and he huffed and puffed in indignation, not used to being insulted. General Otto von Wolfgang led by fear and dominance. He always commanded respect from subordinates and nobles, kings and queens, and generals from foreign armies, for he had never been beaten in any battle he had led. No one ever dared to speak without respect to Otto von Wolfgang.

Greco observed the confrontation from a distance, enjoying every minute of it. He was waiting for the gold to appear to ransom the brothers. He had the pledge of fifty Serbian mercenaries to help him take the gold and head to France. Greco wanted revenge for being humiliated at the DeFusco fortress a few years earlier. Since being defeated in a fight with the Dark Prince for trying to steal jewelry and banished from Naples by Mattiano DeFusco, regent of Naples, Greco had been seething with anger. In forty-nine fights to the death, he never had been defeated, and he remained the undisputed leader in the Poor Soldiers Guild of Sicily. He believed in physical power as the answer to life, for he had never experienced love and human compassion. The Dark Prince easily had defeated him but had not killed him. Greco could not accept it. He would have preferred to go down fighting and die rather than be reminded of the Dark Prince's benevolence. His pride had been crushed.

The Dark Prince leaned forward in his saddle and said to the general, "Bring forth my relatives so I may see them. If any are harmed, I will kill you."

The general felt a shudder go through him as he looked into the eyes of the Dark Prince. "Bring the prisoners forth," the general ordered.

All turned to watch several soldiers bring forth the DeFusco brothers from the German encampment. The prisoners were all chained together as they shuffled toward the Dark Prince of Naples. The brothers had been beaten, especially Mattiano, regent of Naples and father to Henry DeFusco. The Dark Prince was furious. He fixed deadly eyes on General Otto von Wolfgang.

The Dark Prince nudged his horse forward until he was within an arm's length of the general. "Release these men immediately," he demanded.

"Not until I receive the gold," responded the general.

"I could end this now," said the prince.

"Not unless you want to see the sunset this day," responded the general.

As the prisoners were brought forth, German knights slowly made their way in position to stop the prince and his knights from returning to their lines.

Arturo spoke softly to Baldassare. "There are German knights behind us. We will have to fight our way out. Stay close to our prince. You know how he gets heroic and will fight an army on his own."

Danner spoke in a low voice to me. "Keep your temper in check, and protect the prince. We will have to fight our way back. Remember your Templar training. We will fight as a team—all of us, including Arturo and hopefully the mighty Baldassare." Danner gave a sign, and Arturo nodded slightly.

The prince turned to the general of the German army and said angrily, "I will have your head for this outrage and what you have done to my father!"

Otto von Wolfgang laughed and replied, "You are just a wolf's head. In all you have done, you have never taken responsibility for your actions. You killed fifteen French ambassadors in individual duels because you think Naples should be governed by Italians and not the French. Do you think the French king, Philip IV, does not hear of this? The king of France, you see, has enough problems with the Crusades, the English, and the Holy See in Rome. That is why I am here. I will quell this rebellion you started and either kill you or take you back to King Philip in chains and receive five thousand gold pieces as my reward, dead or alive."

The Dark Prince replied, "I stayed on at Acre, the Templar fortress in the desert, while it was under siege. You do remember the fortress, do you not? Your Teutonic knights left a month earlier, like thieves in the middle of the night. Where were you and your fearless, brave knights? We could have used them and held on to Acre. A lot of good men died because of you and your cowardly knights."

Otto von Wolfgang would not look the Dark Prince in the eye. He was ashamed and did not answer.

The Dark Prince made a prearranged hand signal to the fortress. Soon after, two wagons pulled by horse teams made their way to the middle of the field of honor.

Suddenly, a large group of horsemen rode hard from the rear of the German lines to intercept the wagons filled with gold. As the riders thundered near, they fired crossbows, hitting all the DeFusco brothers still in chains. The brothers did not have a chance and were all killed. The Dark Prince was hit and swayed in his saddle. Everyone was surprised by the vicious attack and blamed the other side for treachery.

Otto von Wolfgang had a look of surprise on his face as the Dark Prince painfully drew his sword and lopped off the general's head in one clean swipe. The general's head rolled in front of one of the German knights' horses and spooked the horse.

Arturo, Baldassare, Danner, and I battled the German knights opposite us in a retaliatory fight. The fighting on horseback was fierce, but the more agile horses of the Italians in close quarters made a difference in the outcome. Arturo the Skillful, Baldassare the Ferocious, Danner the Deadly, and I, Tristan the Basher, emerged through the deadly fighting to form up with the wounded prince in the center. We charged through the line of knights who had moved up behind us while the prince and the general were discussing terms. Danner, Baldassare, and I led the charge, with Arturo leading the prince's horse, as the Dark Prince, bleeding and weak, slumped down, barely hanging on to his horse.

Each side blamed the other. The Italians thought the general was not good at his word to release the prisoners; he just wanted the gold. The Germans thought the Italians wanted to renege on the agreement and take back the gold.

*

In all the confusion, Greco made a clean getaway with the fifty Serbian mercenaries and the gold. His plan was to go to France, where the Templar knights were considered evil and disavowed from the church. The Dark Prince of Naples was dead, as were all the DeFusco brothers. Greco felt good. He would have a fine home with servants. No one would look down at him anymore. He would be rich. He would even be a noble now that he had gold. Greco smiled as he thought, *I will live the good life now. I will be giving the orders. Nobles will bend a knee to me. Yes, I will enjoy this good life.*

CHAPTER 18

GRECO'S WORST FEAR

A Serbian mercenary burst into Greco's villa. He was breathless and showed fear in his face as he rushed past servants and other mercenaries till he came to where Greco was sitting at a table, eating a hunk of cheese, dried fish, grapes, and some bread. Wine was nearby. "What is it, Darko?" asked Greco.

Darko replied excitedly, "My lord, friends spotted a small army of maybe one hundred fifty men about three miles away."

Greco replied calmly, "We have stayed clear of politics. No one bothers us. This is not my concern."

Darko replied, "My lord Greco, there are Templar knights, along with people in black scouting to the front and both flanks. We know who is close friends with the Templars and Assassins. The prince still lives and is hunting you down! I killed the Dark Prince with my crossbow. Maybe he is the devil, as the Assassins claim!"

Greco was visibly shaken by the news. He had fled to France because the French king, Philip IV, had a price on the Dark Prince's head, and the Templar knights have fallen out of favor with the French king Philip IV due to politics. Greco stood up, saying, "We have to leave immediately! Gather the men. We will go to the French fortress. They have five thousand men there. The Dark Prince, the heathen Assassins, and the dreaded Templar knights cannot reach us inside the fortress. We have enough gold to bribe the commander of the fortress. Besides, we have done a few favors for him. He owes us."

CHAPTER 19

THE DARK PRINCE OF NAPLES MEETS THE BLACK PRINCE OF ENGLAND

On a rainy day, one of the Assassins came running into the Dark Prince's camp. The Dark Prince and Tamir met with the out-of-breath Assassin to hear what he had to say. Abul spoke softly to the prince and Tamir, saying, "I have seen a great army of many soldiers and knights heading this way! They carry the flag of the English."

The prince looked at Tamir in astonishment and said, "The English! What are they doing here? How many soldiers did you say they have?"

The Assassin replied, "Too many to count! Maybe six thousand or more men."

"How far away are they?" asked the prince.

The Assassin replied, "Maybe three or four days away. They move quickly for such a large army."

*

"Uncle Tristan, what did Grandfather do?" asked Franco.

Mark Anthony was excited and said, "I bet our grandfather fought the English and defeated them and then took the French fort!"

Rose Marie said, "Surely our grandfather the Dark Prince retreated and waited to see what would happen."

Franco said, "No, our grandfather sent the Assassins into the fortress to kill Greco!"

Mark Anthony quickly replied, "The Assassins could do anything! They went in. I know it!"

Rose Marie said quietly, "Uncle Tristan, please tell us. What happened next?"

I had another glass of wine and continued.

*

The Dark Prince was surprised at the news and paused to think about what would be best for his men. Finally, he said, "Bring in all the Assassins. Bring in the Templar knights and all our rangers. We will be at full force when we meet the English. They can be an ally to us. When we are gathered together, I will tell all the men the rules we will go by so as not to provoke the English."

Later that evening, when all the men were assembled, the Dark Prince stood forth and addressed his men. "Loyal knights, bowmen, rangers, and Assassins, as you all know from the rumors you have heard in camp, an English army is heading this way and should arrive here the day after next. We will meet this army as friends, not as enemies. I do not want anyone to act in provocation or threaten these English." The prince turned to Tamir and said, "Tamir, explain to your men what I have just said."

As Tamir was explaining in their language, Arturo and the mighty Baldassare exchanged looks that spoke volumes. Brother Danner and I remained stoic while watching the other warriors react to the prince.

Early the next morning, the Dark Prince and Brother Danner were engrossed in deep conversation. I watched from a distance and realized something was going to happen when the Dark Prince and Brother Danner were involved in conversation. The camp was beginning to come to life. The murmurs of conversation began as men slowly woke up. Fires were lit, and knights and soldiers milled around them. I left my tent and watched Brother Danner race off on his magnificent black stallion on an urgent errand for the prince.

*

Midmorning of the next day, Brother Danner, carrying a white flag of truce, met an English advancement from their main army. Sir Hugo Blackthorn, an English knight, rode up to challenge Brother Danner.

"Halt!" bellowed Sir Hugo, holding one arm up. "State your business, and be quick about it!" Sir Hugo rode to within ten feet of Brother Danner. He was wearing full armor and had his sword drawn and his shield up. His warhorse was snorting and stamping the ground. Horse and rider were impressive to behold.

Brother Danner said, "I come in peace. My name is Danner du Montfort, son of Simon du Montfort, the fifth earl of Leicester, right hand and vicar-general to Charles of Anjou in Tuscany." Brother Danner tucked the white flag into its pouch attached to the saddle. "I am adviser to the prince of Naples, Henry DeFusco. I seek an audience with King Edward of England on behalf of Prince Henry DeFusco."

Sir Hugo nodded slightly in acknowledgment but said, "No one passes by me, by order of my king!"

Brother Danner replied, "Stand aside, knight, and let me pass. If not, I will pass with or without your permission!"

Soldiers behind Sir Hugo heard every word of the exchange with gathered apprehension. They had seen the prowess of Sir Hugo in battle; he was the envy of every English knight there. This newly arrived knight was not impressed with Sir Hugo. He had a certain confidence about him that was neither brash nor boastful. This new knight had the mark of danger about him.

The English soldiers watched as the two knights separated until they were one hundred feet apart. Each raised a sword arm to the other and then charged with sword pointed. There was a clanging of steel to shield, and then they separated for a moment and battled on horseback. The black stallion of Sir Danner du Montfort was far quicker than the mount of Sir Hugo. The ringing of steel on steel brought other English soldiers. They knew Sir Hugo but were interested in the knight Sir Danner du Montfort, who seemed to be the better of the two.

After a time, Sir Hugo called for time, and Sir Danner obliged. Sir Hugo wanted to fight on foot, complaining that Sir Danner had an unfair advantage with his horse. The knights unmounted and approached each other. The English soldiers were uneasy with their champion. The skills of Sir Danner were remarkable. The English soldiers began to make bets as to the outcome.

The two knights closed in with swords clashing and shields banging. Sir Danner was wearing chain mail and moved much faster than Sir Hugo. Sir Danner swung heavy blows to Sir Hugo's helmet, limiting the visibility of Sir Hugo. Sir Danner du Montfort was not trying to kill Sir Hugo. The English soldiers understood how the fight was going. Sir Hugo was taking a beating, but his pride made him go on. Soon it was all over as Sir Danner gave a tremendous sword blow to the helmet of Sir Hugo, splitting it and causing Sir Hugo to collapse.

The English soldiers were stunned. They looked at one another in disbelief. Sir Danner bent down to remove the helmet of the downed Sir Hugo. Slowly, the English soldiers gathered around the fallen knight as Sir Danner tried to give aid. There was a bad gash on Sir Hugo's forehead. Blood was freely flowing from the wound. Sir Hugo's face and head showed painful marks of the bashing he had received. He had been knocked senseless and would take time to recover. Sir Danner ordered a litter to be made for the fallen knight, and the soldiers obeyed.

Later, Sir Danner du Montfort made his way into the English camp, escorted by two of the English soldiers. Sir Danner was on his black stallion, guiding the warhorse dragging the litter carrying Sir Hugo Blackthorn.

There was much commotion as English soldiers and knights surrounded Sir Danner du Montfort, questioning what had happened to Sir Hugo and who Sir Danner du Montfort was. Sir Danner was roughly escorted to King Edward's tent. Many knights gathered to hear what had happened to Sir Hugo.

*

Inside the tent, King Edward listened to his advisers and a recount of events by one of the English soldiers.

"This French knight rides in from nowhere, carrying a white flag of truce; challenges my best knight and defeats him; and then brings my knight to me and demands an audience with me?" bellowed King Edward. "Outrageous!" He kicked a stool, punched a pillow, and then stood abruptly and pointed to one of the soldiers who had accompanied the knight. "Why did you and the others not drag him down and kill him?"

The terrified soldier stammered, saying, "He is a knight, sire, and his father is Simon du Montfort, the fifth earl of Leicester, right hand and vicar-general to Charles of Anjou in Tuscany! You know this man!"

The king paced back and forth in his tent. It was obvious he did not want to meet the foreign knight. The king's audience looked in wonder at King Edward, who was known as the Black Prince because of the black armor he always wore in battle. He was a brave and courageous king, always leading by example. Why was he so afraid of the knight Danner du Montfort?

In early May 1264, Simon du Montfort had marched out to give battle to King Henry of England and scored a spectacular triumph at the Battle of Lewes on May 14, 1264, capturing King Henry; his son, Prince

Edward; and Richard of Cornwall, Henry's brother and the titular king of Germany.

Edward hated Simon du Montfort and his entire family for the defeat at Lewes. He never had gotten over it. Even though Simon du Montfort was living in England and was part of the English government, Edward hated him. Sir Simon had forced King Henry to give up his powers, and King Henry now had to go before a council for approval of what he wanted to do as king. The council kept King Henry in check. Edward had been scheming with other nobles to get rid of Sir Simon and do away with the council.

Had Danner du Montfort found out about his plotting against his father, Sir Simon du Montfort? Danner du Montfort was known throughout Europe as a man to be reckoned with. Sir Danner was a hired mercenary whose prowess in battle was redoubtable. He had disappeared for a time. King Edward had heard rumors that Sir Danner fought in the Crusades as a Templar knight and also fought in Naples, Italy, against a German host, helping Prince Henry DeFusco defeat the invading army. What if the father, Sir Simon du Montfort, had an army nearby? King Edward was afraid of what Sir Danner stood for and what he wanted.

"Tell Sir Danner du Montfort I am busy and cannot see him today. Have him make an appointment with my adviser in a month, when I will return to England," said the king in a peevish voice. The men in the tent were amazed at the king's behavior.

The adviser was turning around to walk out of the tent to relay the message, when Sir Danner burst into the tent. Angrily, he said, "Why have I been forced to wait outside for so long for your king to see me?"

Everyone in the tent jumped back at the sudden appearance of Sir Danner. King Edward moved behind one of his soldiers as if to hide.

Sir Danner scanned the tent, and his eyes settled on the king. He strode up to the king and said in a powerful voice, "I am tired of waiting for an audience with you, Cousin, and demand that you hear what I have to say!"

Everyone was stunned by Sir Danner's actions and the way he addressed King Edward. Sir Danner had already sized up the king and remembered his father, Sir Simon du Montfort, defeating King Henry and his son, Prince Edward. Sir Danner had been there, helping his father and leading the left flank of the army to surround and defeat his cousin Prince Edward and his soldiers. Sir Danner had seen the hatred of the king and son when they were defeated.

"How goes the business of being king?" said Sir Danner to the cowering King Edward.

King Edward tried to regain his composure, courage, and pride in front of his fellow Englishmen in the tent. He replied after a time, "I find it amusing when I am confronted with a peasant dressed in the manner of a knight with all the manners of a dirty pig!"

"Careful, Cousin. You should remind yourself as to your side of the family being raised from the loins of a donkey that bred with a monkey!" replied Sir Danner.

The men in the tent could not contain themselves. Some soldiers laughed, while some of the nobles tittered. The ones who did neither were frightened that there would be bloodshed between Sir Danner and King Edward; they did not want to be caught between them.

The two cousins laughed and hugged, greeting each other in a warriors' grip of friendship.

All the tension in the king's tent vanished. Smiles appeared, and all seemed friendly and warm as the two cousins went arm in arm, talking to each other and laughing about some incident or prank they had played as children. The two found chairs, where they continued telling stories punctuated with laughter. King Edward ordered wine to be brought to them, along with some meats, cheese, and a table.

"What are you doing here in the Aquitaine?" asked King Edward. He filled his goblet with wine and drank from it.

Sir Danner replied, "I am adviser to Prince Henry DeFusco of Naples. We tracked a man named Greco, who killed the prince's father, Mattiano

DeFusco, regent of Naples. My prince wants a justice killing. Greco is hiding in the French fortress not far from here. He also has Serbian mercenaries protecting him."

King Edward drank some more wine as he thought about what Sir Danner had said. He reached for some meat and cheese and placed them on his plate. "I do not believe in coincidence. I am here with my army to retake the Aquitaine, and you appear out of nowhere. You and your family also have French connections, do you not? After all, your family is French but living in England."

Sir Danner drank some wine from the goblet given to him and said, "Cousin, I am not here to spy on you or your army. We have been tracking Greco for a long time. My prince wants justice and will do the killing. My prince wants the gold back that Greco stole. It was a ransom payment for Regent Mattiano."

King Edward smiled. "So there is gold in this story you are telling me. How much gold?"

Sir Danner replied, "Two wagons full."

"Then why are you not storming the fortress to recover the gold and take care of this Greco character? I would. It does not take a scholar to figure this out," King Edward sarcastically responded. The king looked around at his trusted knights and advisers in the tent, smiling. The men in the tent chortled and snorted. Some gave hearty guffaws. King Edward stabbed at some roasted meat with his dagger and chewed. Looking around at his men with a big smile, he said, "Did I help you solve this problem you have?"

"Cousin, my father, Sir Simon du Montfort, and I do not wish to take the fortress ourselves. We have a ten-thousand-man army made up of Italian knights, foot soldiers, and bowmen. We do not want to usurp your right to the Aquitaine. But if you cannot take the fortress with your army, we will help you with our army. After all, are we not of the same blood, Cousin?"

King Edward choked on the meat he was eating, and his knights and advisers muttered about the news of Simon du Montfort's larger army nearby. King Edward looked pale and was no longer jovial. His men looked at one another, terrified and aghast.

King Edward stammered, "My scouts have not reported to me or my trusted knights any army in these parts. How can this be?" He looked quickly at his men, searching in their eyes for any news he was not aware of. They only shook their heads with fear in their eyes.

"Cousin, did you not learn from the last time we met on the battlefield at Lewes that your army is deficient and lacking in certain skills to win in battle?" replied Sir Danner calmly. Sir Danner spied a nice piece of roasted fowl and stabbed it with his dagger to bring to his plate to eat. He became a rock in the storm of fear and tribulations inside the tent as king, advisers, and knights all spoke at once. Sir Danner ignored the din around him as he enjoyed his meat, wine, and cheese.

Late in the day, Sir Danner du Montfort rode away from the English encampment to return to the Dark Prince. King Edward was furiously yelling at all his advisers when Sir Danner left the king's tent. Danner smiled as he remembered the king's face when the king learned that Sir Simon du Montfort had a large army nearby and was awaiting the outcome of the contested French fortress. That big white lie probably had saved Sir Danner's life, as there was no love between King Edward and Sir Danner and his father. Edward always had been a schemer and would be till the day he died.

CHAPTER 20

THE SIEGE

King Edward met with the French commander, Captain Jules Laurent, and his second, Lieutenant Bertrand. They could not come to terms. The French would not surrender the fortress.

Three days later, King Edward commenced his siege on the French fortress that had command of the Aquitaine. Three catapults were in position—two mangonel and the more powerful trebuchet. All three catapults were loaded with large stones that took three or four men to load.

At first, the catapults did not show much damage against the fortress walls, but on the second day of the siege, cracks were showing in the walls. Later in the afternoon, a major breach in one of the walls suddenly appeared. The English soldiers cheered. King Edward ordered them to use a battering ram on the entrance of the fortress, away from where the catapults were striking.

Serbian mercenaries appeared on the ramparts and used their crossbows to counter the battering ram. The crossbows were effective and caused many injuries and deaths to the English using the battering ram. The next attack of the battering ram was met with flaming oil poured down onto the English, who made no further attacks on the entrance to the fortress that day.

On the third day, King Edward, who was furious that he had been stopped for two days, used a variation of Greek fire in pots and hot tar to burn the ramparts and crack the masonry and stone in the walls. The approach was extraordinarily successful and cleared the crossbow men from the ramparts. King Edward had to wait until the fires burned out to launch a strike into the huge breach that had opened.

The king ordered archers to rush to either side of the breach and fire four volleys of arrows at the French inside to panic the French massed to protect the opening. The English followed up with a charge of mounted knights to cut down the massed French. The English foot soldiers soon followed into the mayhem of close-quarters combat. After two hours of back-and-forth fighting, the French surrendered.

Sir Danner, the Dark Prince, Arturo, Baldassare, Ravenaire, and I rode down from a distant hill we had been on to observe the battle. Sir Danner rode forward from the rest of us and said to King Edward, "Congratulations on your victory."

King Edward smiled and said, "Who are these people? Please introduce them to me."

After introductions, King Edward said to the prince, "I have met a few Italians and have found them to be buffoons or rapscallions. Which are you?"

The Dark Prince smiled and answered, "Neither."

King Edward looked to Sir Danner and then turned away and addressed Sir Baldassare. "Sir Big Fellow, who do you think is the better swordsman—Sir Danner or your prince?"

Sir Baldassare held back his growing temper and replied, "My prince is the better swordsman."

The king looked to Sir Arturo and asked, "Why do you think your prince is the better swordsman?"

Sir Arturo replied, "Unless you live under a rock, the jousting records in Europe will show my prince has won them all. I have not seen your name listed."

Danner made a certain prearranged sign, and on a distant hill, mounted cavalry appeared, covering the top and both slopes of the hill.

King Edward caught Sir Danner looking off into the distance, followed his gaze, and said, "I see Simon du Montfort's army on that distant hill."

Everyone turned to look at the mounted soldiers lining the distant hilltop. Many commented on what a large and glorious army it was.

The Dark Prince said, "Stand aside, King Edward. I have unfinished business at the fortress."

King Edward started to fuss and fume at being spoken to that way, when suddenly, he was at sword point from the Dark Prince, who said, "Do you want to see which of us is the better swordsman and which of us is the buffoon?"

King Edward replied in a shaky voice, "Left-handed is the devil's hand side! I must see to my men. Do what you want before sundown."

Up on the hilltop, the Dark Prince had all his knights, the Templar knights, and the Assassins wearing pails on their heads to simulate armored helmets and holding up broomsticks and staffs to replicate lances from a distance as a bluff to Edward of Simon du Montfort's large army. The line they made was only one man deep and spread out over the hill. Two men were behind the line, banging pots and making metallic noises to replicate the movement of men in armor. They yelled out various commands to further enhance the charade. It worked.

The Dark Prince said, "Bring forth Scipio and the wolf dog. The wolf dog will help us locate Greco and whoever else is protecting him."

The Dark Prince and his companions, of whom I was one, proceeded to the smoking fortress as soon as Scipio and the wolf dog arrived. At the fortress, we all dismounted, and the Dark Prince ordered Scipio and the wolf dog to go before us and enter the rooms beneath the fortress. Our small company started to systematically look through all the rooms, led by Scipio and the wolf dog. We searched room after room, until we came to a locked door late in the day. The wolf dog growled, scratching at the floor in front of the door.

The Dark Prince ordered everyone back to discuss our next move. I said softly, "We can have Baldassare break in the door and rush them."

The Dark Prince replied, "What about the crossbow men? We know he had many of them, and I doubt they all perished from the Greek fire and burning tar on the ramparts."

We all thought some more.

Finally, the Dark Prince said, "We can burn the door down. The smoke will act as a cover to us while choking those inside. We will go in with shields out front to protect us against possible crossbows. Ravenaire, you stay back. This is dangerous business."

Ravenaire replied, "I go where my husband goes!"

The men in the company shrugged when the Dark Prince looked at each one for confirmation.

We set fire to the bottom of the door and watched the flames spread higher. Smoke started to billow up toward the ceiling as we continued to feed the flames with debris from the recent battle. When the door weakened and was about to fall off its hinges, the Dark Prince ordered a charge with shields up. The wolf dog and Scipio slipped in first before the rest of us. Through the smoke and fire, the wolf dog found one of the Serbian mercenaries and attacked. The man screamed out in pain as the wolf dog dragged him down. Baldassare rushed right behind Scipio, grabbed two mercenaries, and slammed their heads together, causing an explosion of gray matter. Arturo caught another mercenary through the chest with his sword, while the Dark Prince looked for Greco.

Greco saw the Dark Prince and threw his knife. Ravenaire stepped in front of the Dark Prince to take the knife in her chest. She staggered for a couple of steps and then slowly slid to the floor. Brother Danner immediately rushed to Ravenaire. In all the commotion of smoke, fire, and close-quarter combat, no one else saw Ravenaire go down. Brother Danner called out to the Dark Prince in a strangulated voice as the Dark Prince closed in on Greco. The Dark Prince stopped immediately, for he had never heard Sir Danner speak like that. He looked to where the voice had come from and recognized Ravenaire lying on the floor. The prince saw blood trickling from the corner of her mouth and the dagger in her chest.

The Dark Prince felt deep anguish as he saw the love of his life lying on the floor with a dagger buried in her chest. Tears streamed down his cheeks, and he was incapacitated. Greco smiled at the loss of Ravenaire and slowly moved in on the Dark Prince to kill him.

Brother Danner called out for me. I immediately dropped the Serbian mercenary I had just dispatched and hurried to where Brother Danner was. As I passed the mighty Baldassare, I said, "Come with me, and shield and protect us. Ravenaire has taken a grievous injury."

We both rushed to Brother Danner. I felt my knees give out when I saw Ravenaire. Brother Danner cradled Ravenaire in his arms.

Brother Danner spoke in a distant voice, asking Baldassare and me to join in the sacred prayer of the Templar knights to rejuvenate Ravenaire's soul. Brother Danner made the sign of the cross, and I quickly followed. We both said sacred Templar incantations.

Brother Danner said quietly to Baldassare, "I want you to pray to God for the salvation of Ravenaire."

Baldassare mumbled, "I do not know how to pray. I have not prayed since I was a little boy. I have forgotten how."

Brother Danner replied, "Talk to God. Let him know how you feel about Ravenaire. Ask him to forgive you and your sins for the love of God in your heart to listen to you. Plead with God for your sorrow. Brother Tristan and I will pray the Templar knights' special prayer for Ravenaire."

Greco found the Dark Prince and slashed at him with his hatchet. The Dark Prince somehow reacted and blocked the vicious swing of the hatchet. Greco was stunned for a moment but recovered quickly enough to grab his dagger from his belt and turn to thrust it. The Dark Prince was fully engaged with the evil Greco, and while blocking the hatchet, he hit Greco with a powerful punch to the nose, causing Greco to stagger backward. The Dark Prince drew his dagger and fought with both sword and dagger.

Greco, who stood six feet three and weighed 310 pounds, was a street fighter. He knew all the tricks to stay alive and had the scars to prove it. He vowed the hated Dark Prince in front of him would die a terrible death.

The Dark Prince had fought many fights with sword and dagger over two continents and was always victorious. His quick and explosive movements and skills with the blade had made him a legend. He and Greco clashed like two mighty beasts of the forest in the swirling smoke of the room. Steel against steel rang out as the two men fought to the death.

Greco was immediately put on the defensive, as the Dark Prince had superior skills and knowledge. Greco swung his hatchet at the prince's head, but the prince blocked it with the flat of his sword and thrust his dagger into Greco twice before moving back. Greco winced. He felt warm blood stream down his chest. Desperately, Greco charged again with hatchet and dagger. A quick slash of the prince's sword to the hand holding the hatchet cleaved it off, and the hand and hatchet fell to the ground. Blood spurted from the stump where Greco's hand had been. Greco backed away, frantically looking for an escape.

The Dark Prince closed in on Greco. Greco tried to slash the prince with his dagger, but the prince was too quick. He slashed Greco in the ribs and belly.

Greco was getting weak, and his knees gave way. He knelt before the Dark Prince and begged for mercy. He told the prince that as a Christian, the prince should let him go. Greco offered the prince gold. He was desperate. He motioned for the prince to come closer so he could tell him something. The prince was alert but moved forward to better hear Greco. Greco moved quickly like a viper to make an upward slash to the groin of the prince. The prince anticipated the move and stepped to the side while plunging his dagger into Greco's neck and giving it a little twist.

Greco had a surprised look on his face. He stayed upright in a kneeling position for a few seconds and then fell forward onto the floor.

The Dark Prince turned, leaving Greco dead on the floor, and saw Arturo with an arrow through his thigh and a bloodied left arm hanging down at his side. He limped over to where Danner was cradling Ravenaire and praying to God. Brother Danner and I were in an intense state of prayer.

The Dark Prince saw that Arturo felt an acute loss for Ravenaire, and with tears streaming down his face, he began praying. The prince saw Baldassare holding his bloody side while kneeling and praying where his companions were. The enormity of the situation hit the Dark Prince hard. He began sobbing as tears flooded his eyes. He was a ferocious man in combat but a sensitive man when not aroused.

Arturo was the first to hear a slight sound of tinkling glass wind chimes. The room took on a slight glow. Blood appeared on Brother Danner's wrists and around his head, as if he wore a crown of thorns and his wrists had been pierced by nails.

Arturo cleared the tears from his eyes and looked again. There was no blood on Sir Danner. Arturo was puzzled and thought he had imagined it. He looked at the Dark Prince, who was still moving his lips in deep prayer with his eyes closed. I was also in deep prayer. Arturo searched out the mighty Baldassare and found him sobbing on his knees, a little away from the rest of us. Arturo started to go to comfort Baldassare, but he stopped suddenly. Ravenaire had opened her eyes and had a look of awe. The dagger was gone from her chest. *The Dark Prince must have pulled it out*, Arturo thought as he moved slowly forward.

Ravenaire looked into the intense face of the Dark Prince and softly said, "I love you, my husband and prince."

The Dark Prince kept his eyes shut and kept praying. I heard Ravenaire and quickly looked to her. Brother Danner smiled and gently nudged the Dark Prince, who ignored him at first. After another nudge, the Dark Prince angrily said, "I am praying, monk. Cannot you give me peace to pray? I am trying to do as you have told me to do many times."

Everyone heard Ravenaire laugh at the interaction between Danner and the Dark Prince. She then said, "My prince, you should try very hard to pray more often. They say it is good for the soul."

The Dark Prince was startled by Ravenaire's voice and looked down at her. She smiled up at him and gave him a deep kiss.

Brother Danner and I rose, smiling. Arturo limped over to the mighty Baldassare, who was still sobbing and had not heard that Ravenaire was alive. Arturo said softly to Baldassare, "I am sorry for our loss of Ravenaire. But our prayers have been answered, and she is alive!"

Baldassare tried to compose himself, wiped away the tears he had shed, and, with wide eyes, looked upon the Dark Prince holding Ravenaire. He laughed.

Shortly, the Dark Prince and Ravenaire rose and joined hands with their companions in prayer to God. We were all jubilant and happy for Ravenaire and for the grace of God.

We looked for Scipio and the wolf dog. I said solemnly, "Over here. I have found them." The group came over and saw Scipio with a dagger in his back. Lying over Scipio was the wolf dog with two arrows in him.

"Even in death, the wolf dog defends him," said Arturo.

Brother Danner said, "The wolf dog has a snarl frozen on his face, with blood still dripping from his fangs."

Arturo said in deep reverence, "The two of them killed eight mercenaries. Look at the knife wounds on the mercenaries' bodies and also the teeth marks from the wolf. Scipio and his wolf both went down fighting."

Baldassare sighed and added, "Someone stabbed Scipio from behind. They could not take him down face-to-face. This must have happened while I was fighting several Serbians. I feel bad for Scipio and his wolf. Maybe I could have helped him."

Arturo said to his cousin, "Baldassare, Scipio would have preferred to go down fighting alongside his wolf. They were an incredible team. Scipio and the wolf would not have wanted any help and would not have died any other way."

Brother Danner led us in prayer for Scipio and the wolf dog. After the prayer, we left the fortress and headed for home. We left with joy for Ravenaire and life. We also felt sorrow for the young Scipio and his wolf.

*

Weeks later, in Naples, Arturo and Baldassare were talking about the events of Ravenaire's death and her return to life. Arturo said, "I swear I saw the monk Danner bleeding from his head and wrists like the crucified Christ! He was even wearing a crown of thorns."

Baldassare smiled and said, "You have a vivid imagination and are much too sensitive to be like me. I always knew Ravenaire would come back to us."

Arturo responded, "Do not let me catch you sobbing again like a little boy who lost a puppy." He playfully punched Baldassare on the shoulder.

Baldassare held his shoulder and said, "Ouch! That hurt! You must be working out to make your flabby, nonexistent muscles stronger."

The cousins laughed and looked to another glorious day in Naples.

*

One year later, Ravenaire gave birth to twin boys. One boy had red hair; the other had curly dark brown hair and could scream louder than his brother. The Dark Prince was happy. He truly became the prince of Naples, and the people loved him as a hero to the people for driving the French out and avenging his father's death. Arturo and Baldassare argued over caring for the two little princes.

Sir Danner looked aged. He now had streaks of gray in his hair and was not as vigorous as he once had been. Arturo felt that the miracle Sir Danner had performed over Ravenaire through his relationship with God had taken a lot out of him. I stayed on to help Sir Danner and learn to be adviser to the prince.

Tamir left for the Middle East with most of the Assassins. He ordered his best Assassins to look after the prince and Ravenaire. Tamir vowed before he left that the prince and Ravenaire's children would always be protected and watched over. Tamir looked forward to their visits in the future.

*

The twins thanked me for telling the story of their grandparents. Mark Anthony and Rose Marie then left the room together and came back shortly, carrying a bundle that rattled as it moved. Franco recognized the bundle, jumped up, and said, "Uncle Tristan, it is time for our practice lessons."

I smiled and said, "Hand me my sword, and prepare to defend yourselves!"

The twins and Rose Marie were all smiles as they picked up their individual wooden swords. The swords were full size and weight. They were not play toys. Rose Marie handed me my wooden sword, and the children went to their spots and waited in anticipation.

I called out, "Franco, you are first! Show me what you have learned." I noticed that Franco showed skills similar to those of his grandfather the Dark Prince.

I smiled as Franco caught me in the ribs with his wooden sword after a flurry of cuts and slashes. Franco kissed the sword hilt, as was the Templar knights' custom in a winning sword stroke.

I smiled and said, "Well done, Franco. Well done."

Mark Anthony was next. He was more of a thinker in his swordplay. I immediately saw that Mark Anthony had improved from our last session, and I thought he was like Arturo in the way he fought.

I let my guard slip. Mark Anthony saw the opening and struck.

I congratulated him. "That was a good move on me, Mark Anthony. Good job. Next time, kiss the sword hilt, as I have shown you. It is a tribute to God for guiding you in combat."

Rose Marie chose her favorite weapons: a sword and dagger. I saluted her with my wooden sword, and she saluted me. She attacked with a ferocity that surprised me. Rose Marie was just like her grandmother. I parried her sword attacks with difficulty while dodging the thrusts of her wooden dagger. After some time, the room was in disarray, for it had become an epic battle.

Rose Marie let her guard down for just a moment, and I made my thrust. "Well done, Rose Marie! Well done. You pressed an old man to the brink of defeat."

Rose Marie bowed and saluted me. The boys applauded the performance and congratulated her.

Rose Marie came over to me and said, "Uncle Tristan, I found a picture of my grandfather that you should use as a cover for your manuscript."

The twin boys and I followed her to another room. Hanging on a wall was a painting of the Dark Prince. We all studied the picture for a short while. I looked hard at the portrait and saw the strength and confidence coming from the man in the picture.

I smiled broadly and said, "This portrait captures the essence of your grandfather. I will gladly have this picture copied by monks I know to add to my manuscript so that people will read this story down through the ages."

Printed in the United States
by Baker & Taylor Publisher Services